WE WERE THE FIRE
BIRMINGHAM 1963

WE WERE THE
FIRE

BIRMINGHAM 1963

SHELIA P. MOSES

 Nancy Paulsen Books

NANCY PAULSEN BOOKS

An imprint of Penguin Random House LLC, New York

First published in the United States of America by Nancy Paulsen Books,
an imprint of Penguin Random House LLC, 2022

Nancy Paulsen Books & colophon are trademarks of
Penguin Random House LLC.

The Penguin colophon is a registered trademark of Penguin Books Limited.

Visit us online at penguinrandomhouse.com.

Library of Congress Cataloging-in-Publication Data
Names: Moses, Shelia P., author.
Title: We were the fire: Birmingham 1963 / Shelia P. Moses.
Description: New York: Nancy Paulsen Books, 2022. | Summary: Determined to
stand up for their rights, eleven-year-old Rufus, a Black boy, and his friends participate
in the 1963 civil rights protests in Birmingham, Alabama.
Identifiers: LCCN 2022016355 | ISBN 9780593407486 (hardcover) |
ISBN 9780593407493 (ebook)
Subjects: CYAC: Segregation—Fiction. | African Americans—Fiction. | Civil rights
demonstrations—Fiction. | Birmingham (Ala.)—History—20th century—Fiction. |
LCGFT: Historical fiction. | Novels.
Classification: LCC PZ7.M8475 We 2022 | DDC [Fic]—dc23
LC record available at https://lccn.loc.gov/2022016355

Printed in the United States of America

ISBN 9780593407486

1 3 5 7 9 10 8 6 4 2

CJKB

Edited by Nancy Paulsen | Design by Suki Boynton
Text set in Hoefler Text

✧

This book is dedicated to my big brother,
Daniel McCoy Moses, and to one of my
greatest teachers, Dick Gregory.

WE WERE THE FIRE
BIRMINGHAM 1963

1

My name is Rufus. Rufus Jackson Jones Jr.

I was born in Birmingham, Alabama.

The place Dr. Martin Luther King Jr. called the most segregated place in the country.

Birmingham is the South. The Deep South! The South is in my soul.

The year that changed my life happened in Birmingham.

It was a year that changed America. Maybe the world. It was 1963.

"Segregation now . . . segregation tomorrow . . .

segregation forever," Governor George Wallace said during his inaugural speech.

I didn't know exactly what his words meant. I was only eleven years old. I just knew what he said was wrong. Each word that came out of his mouth made my sweet mama's smile turn into a frown.

After the death of my daddy, Rufus Sr., hard times had taken away her joy. My mama, Tillie Jones, worked hard at home and even harder at Boone's Steel Mill. Mama worked in the kitchen there, where the men lined up to eat the good meals the colored women cooked. Mama's brother, Uncle Sam, was the only colored manager at the steel mill. He had a college degree, and white folks looked at him a little different than most colored folks. They showed him respect. Not enough—but more than most colored folks. They still called him Sam, not Mr. Lewis, while calling white managers "Mr. This" and "Mr. That." Uncle Sam had to sit in the colored section when he ate lunch, just like Mama. When he entered the building, he walked in the back door, just like Mama.

One day, Uncle Sam and the other colored folks in Birmingham got real tired of back doors. They were tired of hard work and low pay, no right to vote, and their children going to raggedy schools with used books. That was when the secret meetings started.

I heard that there were going to be all kinds of

protests. But it was going to be hard fighting people like Bull Connor, who was in control of the police—folks said he was also a member of the Ku Klux Klan. Colored folks in Birmingham feared Bull Connor like the plague. I knew about Bull Connor because I read about him in the newspaper. We could not afford the paper, but Uncle Sam passed his newspaper on to my mama at work every day, and I'd read it when she was done. My aunt Ola was always bringing me old *Jet* and *Ebony* magazines. That is how I learned about Dr. Martin Luther King Jr. and Reverend Fred Shuttlesworth. My teacher, Miss Smith, told us they were important leaders. She said we were important too.

Uncle Sam agreed with them that now was the time to act. He was real smart, and so was Aunt Ola. They got married right after they graduated from Shaw University. She was a high school English teacher and fancy in the way she talked, walked, and dressed, but she wasn't snobby about it. She and Mama were not just sisters-in-law, but they were also best friends.

All Mama's other friends worked at the steel mill or spent their days cooking and cleaning for white people. They carpooled or walked to the white neighborhoods to earn just three dollars a day, and then they rushed home before dark. No colored woman—or man—was safe in Birmingham after the sun went down.

We lived in a place called Bull Hill. A place where the houses were all raggedy and owned by a white man named Smarty Hanks, who couldn't have been stingier. Each house had two tiny bedrooms, a sitting area, and a small kitchen. Not one house had been painted since anyone could remember, and a lot of our porches looked like they were ready to fall down.

Everyone on Bull Hill shopped at the same grocery store, and all us kids got bused to a colored school downtown. Mama said when she was a little girl, the folks on Bull Hill had a one-room schoolhouse for the colored children. It had dirt floors and no running water.

Come Sunday morning, everyone put on their Sunday best to praise God at one of the many colored churches in Birmingham. Churches like 16th Street Baptist Church. Mama loved that church best. She sang in the women's choir, but every now and then someone would ask her to sing at another church. She would go, but she rarely missed a Sunday at her own church.

"I feel close to my own mama and papa when I walk in the doors of 16th Street," Mama would say every Sunday morning. Her mama and daddy died before I was born, but Mama talked about them like they were sitting on the bench right beside us. They had moved here when Mama was a little girl from a little town called Rich Square, North Carolina, to work in the steel mill.

My daddy and some of his folks came to Birmingham for the same reason. Daddy said it beat working in the cotton fields.

Mama loved her mama and daddy with all her heart, and now she loves me and my sister, Georgia, the same way. I was born a couple of years before Georgia, and even though I like to tease her, she knows I love her. Georgia's quiet and gentle like Mama, while I'm more like my daddy. Folks that knew him always say that he was a lion of a man with a fighting spirit that he left inside of me. I tried to fill his shoes the best way I knew how. But his shoes were big. And first I had to see if I could even fill the hole in my heart from missing him.

I was nine years old when my daddy fell from the ladder at the mill and died. It was just before Christmas in 1960. Uncle Sam drove Mama home from the mill that day so she could deliver the news to us that Daddy was gone. I hugged her tight on one side, and Georgia hugged the other.

Mama didn't say another word after she told us Daddy had met his maker. She did what she always did when her heart was hurting—sing.

I can still hear her singing Daddy's favorite song.

"Precious Lord, take my hand. Lead me on . . ."

She sang to the heavens as Georgia's tiny little voice joined hers.

I never opened my mouth. I just kept squeezing Mama as tight as I could.

When the house filled up with cakes, pies, Bull Hill folks, and more tears, I ran to my room. I used my finger to write one word on the cold glass windowpane.

Daddy was the only word in my heart.

2

Mama had too much pride to accept help from our neighbors—or even from our family.

Uncle Sam tried to get us to move into the well-to-do Smithfield neighborhood where he lived so we'd be close to him and Aunt Ola. He even offered to buy Mama a house and let us live there, but Mama said no. She said Bull Hill was safer for us than Smithfield. Coloreds called the Smithfield area that was over on Center Street "Dynamite Hill" because the white folk would get so mad every time a Negro moved in that they'd throw bombs at their houses.

So we settled into a lonely life without Daddy, but not for long. The following year, a man named Paul Joe Peele showed up.

Mr. Paul was as dark as our potbelly stove—and he wasn't much taller. But he was still a big man, and his muscles jumped in his neck every time he laughed. He moved back to our neighborhood from Chicago to live in his childhood home with his sister, Miss Maggie, because folks said his wife loved other menfolks. That was the gossip on Bull Hill.

Mr. Paul was good friends with Uncle Sam all the way back to elementary school, so my uncle helped him get a job at the steel mill. On Sundays after church, they'd talk in the parking lot about baseball, Dr. Martin Luther King, protesting, and stuff like that. Me and my best friends, Slide and YouOut, would hang around nearby and try to listen.

Slide's real name was Curtis Wilkins, but we called him Slide because no one could slide into home base on the baseball field like he could. He lived next door to us with his mama, Miss Annie Ruth, and his daddy, Mr. Jack. YouOut's real name was Ronnie Spivey, but we called him YouOut because he could strike you out in a blink of an eye. Then he would shout, "You out!" He had big dreams to be an umpire one day. We all loved baseball, and someday I wanted to write about sports and the colored people who played them.

The more I heard about the movement, the more I wanted to know. It seemed like all folks talked about these days was marching, voting, and getting off of raggedy Bull Hill. We learned a lot listening to Uncle Sam and Mr. Paul. But I also noticed that while Mr. Paul had one eye on the movement, he had the other one on my mother.

Every Sunday after church and talking in the parking lot, Mr. Paul showed up at our front door with flowers for Mama and dessert for me and Georgia.

In my whole life I had never known my mama to lie, but when Mr. Paul knocked on the door . . . the sinning started.

"Tell him I'm not home," she whispered to me and Georgia the first Sunday Mr. Paul showed up.

"Mr. Paul, Mama said to tell you she ain't home," Georgia shouted from the living room.

"Well, you tell her that I'll wait for her," he shouted back.

"Okay." Georgia looked at Mama and said, "You hear that?" and then went back to playing with her dolls, which were lined up as if they were her students. The dolls were all white because Mama wasn't able to find any colored dolls in Birmingham.

Then I opened the door just wide enough to get our

dessert. "Thank you for the pie, Mr. Paul," I said real quick.

He came back the following Sunday, and every Sunday after that. After eating a slice of that week's pie, we'd peek out the window to make sure Mr. Paul was still breathing. No matter how hot it got that summer of '62, he'd sit in Daddy's rocking chair and rock.

Some Sundays Mr. Paul would still be sitting there when I'd go out into the front yard to play baseball with Slide and the other Bull Hill boys.

"Why is Mr. Paul on your porch every Sunday?" Slide asked one day.

"Who knows, but Mama ain't thinking about him," I whispered.

I didn't like him sitting in my daddy's chair, but I did feel sorry for him.

Sunday after Sunday poor Mr. Paul came over to see our mama. Sunday after Sunday she would send him home. But one Sunday our mama had a change of heart and surprised us all by going to the door herself and saying, "Paul, come on in and have dinner with us."

Mr. Paul was as happy as a tick on a dog as he rushed inside.

When Mama put dinner on the table, he looked at the food and then he looked at Mama.

"Tillie, I ate too much breakfast. Y'all eat. I will just have some pie."

"Now, Paul, you welcome to have some chicken and collard greens. I even made some cornbread."

"Thank you, but I should probably eat with Maggie later," Mr. Paul said.

I was ten and a half by then, but I had enough sense to know why he didn't eat. He could see Mama didn't have enough food. So he smiled and ate pie while we filled our bellies.

After that day Mr. Paul came every Sunday. He started stopping by on Saturdays too so he could drop off a ham or chicken. He knew Mama liked cooking on Saturday night while she sang along to gospel music on the radio.

We relied on the radio for the news too, since our little television had stopped working right after daddy died and Mama said we couldn't afford a new one. I secretly prayed Mr. Paul would bring us a television one day and wondered if Mama would take it. Uncle Sam had tried to give us one of theirs, but Mama refused. Her pride meant no cartoons on Saturday morning.

Soon Mr. Paul was dropping things off lots of days of the week. Mornings we would wake up and a whole mess of collards would be on our front porch. Some days a watermelon or cantaloupe would be blocking the door. Whatever Mr. Paul left, he would put a flower from the yard on top.

The flowers would change with the seasons, but not Mr. Paul. He stayed the same—except he did finally started eating with us after he had filled the icebox and the cupboards with food. Every Sunday after dinner he would stand up, clear his throat, and say the same thing. "Tillie, dinner sho' was good. Now come sit on the porch with me awhile." And Mama would join Mr. Paul on the porch till sundown.

One Sunday I waited and waited, but he didn't get up from the table. Just before I swallowed my last bite of lemon pie, Mr. Paul stood up. Then he started to go down on one knee. I thought he was having a heart attack.

"You all right, Paul? Get him some water, Georgia," Mama shouted, but Paul shook his head. He looked fine. That's when I realized he was not having a heart attack, but he was about to give me and Georgia one.

"Marry me, Tillie," he said. "I love you. Let me help take care of you and your children. Let me love you, Georgia, and Rufus."

Mama looked at me. Then she looked at Georgia as my little sister jumped up and sat herself down in our own daddy's chair, where Mr. Paul had just been sitting.

"Lord have mercy, Paul. I can't marry you. I still got love in my heart for my husband. My children got his blood in their veins."

"I don't want to hear about blood. I am talking about love. Love that's alive, Tillie. We are alive. I love you and your children like they my own. I knew Rufus Sr. in school, and I know he was a good man. He'd want his children taken care of. You will be all right with me, Tillie. Marry me," Mr. Paul begged.

"How can I marry you when you already got a wife—a mean wife, I hear—and she might show up any day?"

"Forget about Marjorie. I'm divorcing her. Everything will be final next week," Mr. Paul said as he got off his knee.

"Paul, the answer is still the same. Now I best clean up so I can help my children with their homework."

"All right. I have to go over to your brother's house now, anyway. Reverend Shuttlesworth says Dr. King and some other civil rights leaders are coming back to Birmingham. We got a lot to talk about. But I will see you at work tomorrow, and yes, I will be back next Sunday and the Sunday after that, okay, Tillie? I love you, and I ain't going to stop asking you to marry me."

"Y'all be careful at your meeting, Paul. That's all I got to say. Be careful."

I watched from the window as Mr. Paul drove away. I was not going to tell Mama, but I was starting to like him. He cared about us, and he wanted white folks in Birmingham to stop treating us so bad. But liking him was one thing; wanting him to marry my mama was another.

Mr. Paul did what he said and came back the next Sunday and the one after that. I guess it was taking Mama too long to say yes, so he must have asked Uncle Sam to come over and put in a good word for him too.

Me and Slide were in the yard playing catch when the grown folks sat down on the porch. I moved closer to hear what they were saying.

"Sister, you ain't getting any younger. Go on and marry Paul. He will be good to you and the children," Uncle Sam told her.

"Mind your business, big brother. I thought you came over to talk to us about plans for the march at Kelly Park."

"Well, I did, but we can talk about more than one thing."

"Can I go to the next meeting?" I asked.

Mama looked at me. "Rufus, please stay out of

grown folks' business . . . and no, you can't go to the meeting."

"He just wants to know what's going on, sister. Don't be so hard on the boy," Uncle Sam said.

"Yeah, don't be so hard on me," I repeated and laughed.

"Don't be a smart mouth, Rufus Jr.," Mama said as she pointed toward the door for me to take my butt into the house. Anytime Mama added *Junior* to my name, I knew I was in trouble. I went inside and didn't get to hear what more my uncle had to say. That was the end of that!

But by the next Sunday, something had changed. Uncle Sam and Mr. Paul brought me and Georgia back to Bull Hill after church was over. Mama and Aunt Ola took a ride in her nice Ford car to visit Daddy at the cemetery. While they were gone, Mr. Paul laid out the smoked ham, turnip greens, and peach cobbler.

When Mama and Aunt Ola walked in the door, Mama looked at me and Georgia with all the love she had in her heart. She flashed her eyes on Paul with that same love. Georgia noticed it too, and she must've known something was about to happen, because tears filled her eyes.

Aunt Ola put her hand on my little sister's shoulder.

Mama's mouth began to move faster than my heartbeat. "I been to the cemetery to have a word with Rufus Sr. He is at peace with God. And he is at peace with us moving on with our lives."

Mr. Paul looked so happy, and we knew what that meant. He smiled at my mama like he had hit the lottery at the corner store downtown.

"Don't say another word, Tillie. I'm going home so you can be with your children," he said as he put on his Chicago-style hat.

"Come on, Ola, we are leaving too," Uncle Sam said as he cut a piece of ham and put it in a napkin.

By the time they had all left, Georgia was crying like she had lost her mind, and I was hot as fish grease—there was no way I wanted him to marry my mama.

"Stop your crying, Georgia," Mama said as she pulled us close to her and sat in between us on our old blue couch. "You got one daddy. Just one. Can't anybody replace Rufus Sr. . . . but he ain't coming back. I want to marry Paul and be happy again. All you got to do is be nice to him. You got to respect him, but you ain't never got to call him Daddy."

"Well, ain't you happy with us?" Georgia asked Mama.

"Yes, of course I'm happy with you. I love you and your brother more than anything. But we can all be happy with Paul too. God put enough love in this family's hearts for one more person. That person is Paul."

Georgia wrapped her arms around Mama's neck and finally stopped crying. "Okay, Mama. I do want you to be real happy."

I gave Mama a big hug. If my little sister could be okay with Mama getting married, then I figured I could too.

3

On her wedding day, Mama looked so pretty in the cream-colored dress she made herself with fabric Aunt Ola gave her as a wedding present.

I decided to give Mama a special wedding gift. I stood in the mirror and practiced saying "Daddy Paul." Not "Daddy"—that was for sure. "Daddy Paul" was hard enough. The words could barely get out of my mouth, but I would say it for Mama's sake.

Uncle Sam picked us up to take us to the ceremony at the church. Seemed like half the folks from Bull Hill had put on their Sunday best to come to the wedding.

Mama held her new husband's hands and sang "Unforgettable" by Nat King Cole. Hearing Mama sing to our new stepdaddy was when I realized that hearts can heal. Mama's voice told me how happy she was.

After the wedding we headed over to Uncle Sam and Aunt Ola's house for the reception. They insisted on paying for everything, and it was mighty fine. Daddy Paul's sister, Miss Maggie, had helped Aunt Ola lay out everything so nice.

Before we ate, I got Georgia to agree to the surprise, and when we opened our lips and said "Daddy Paul" for the first time, I swear the vein in my new daddy's neck jumped, and he smiled so big that it made us smile. To add frosting to the cake, we started calling his sister Aunt Maggie.

"Y'all some sweet children," Aunt Maggie said as she hugged us tight. "Now let's dance!" She pulled us to the floor as Slide's daddy, Mr. Jack, played Nat King Cole's "Let There Be Love" on the record player.

In between dancing and eating, Slide and I listened to the grown folks talking more about Dr. King and other leaders coming to town. It was happening soon.

"There's going to be trouble when Bull Connor gets word that the high school students are going to join our march," Uncle Sam said.

"We can't get in any more trouble than we in," Daddy Paul said. "Project C is going to stir this town up, so we best be ready for lots more trouble."

"High school children are marching too!" I whispered to Slide as we moved away from the grown-ups.

"I know," Slide said. "Remember? YouOut's brother Junie said he's gonna march with all his high school friends. You think that means we can march one day?"

"I sure hope so. I've been reading in the paper about Project C. Reverend Shuttlesworth says it's gonna show the country how unfair segregation is," I told Slide. "There'll be lots of sit-ins and marches and protests. I bet they need plenty of us to help."

"Well, they probably ain't going to let kids our age march, so we got to come up with our own plan. That's what Junie told YouOut."

Slide and I talked about our plans to *make* plans as we got ourselves another piece of wedding cake. We knew our day would come.

⚜

Around the same time we got a stepdaddy, it looked like we might be getting a new home too.

Uncle Sam hadn't stopped pestering Mama about

moving near him, and now he was trying to convince Daddy Paul too.

"I ate lunch with Sam at the mill yesterday," Daddy Paul said at dinner about a month after he and Mama were married. "You know I don't want to move to Smithfield either, but I'd like us to move."

"Where we moving to?" Georgia asked.

"Well, I heard the guys at the mill talking about Miss Boone, who owns the mill. She got an empty house on her land over there in Ivy Town. It's way back in the woods, but it will be fine for now—and it's better than this place. The houses there are old too, but they have heat, running water, and a bathroom. A few white families who work at the mill been living back there for years. And I heard there's a colored family back there too."

"That's right, husband. It's home to mostly poor white folks. Ain't no colored folks I know living in Ivy Town. And ain't no schools for us for miles and miles. Besides, Miss Boone could have stepped in and helped get Rufus Sr.'s insurance check for the children, but she didn't. Why you think she going to help now?"

"Now, wife, this is Birmingham! *Nothing* is for colored folks for miles and miles. It don't hurt to ask Miss Boone. If she says yes, we can get up early and drive the children to school. Besides, isn't it time to desegregate more of this town? When we leave church tomorrow, we gonna stop by and ask her," Daddy Paul said.

"I don't know," Mama said. "I think I'd rather live near my brother than in a white folks' neighborhood. Seems like we'd be safer with the folks who already started integrating an area."

"Listen! Somebody got to be the first or second person to move into these white neighborhoods. Integration is hard, but someone got to do it. We going to be the second to move to Ivy Town." Daddy Paul looked at us. "Do y'all know what *integration* means?"

"I know! I know!" I said. "Miss Smith says it means to unite people of different races so they can have equal rights."

Mama seemed pleased that I was learning so much at school, but she was still scared of Ivy Town.

Daddy Paul spoke up. "Look, I wish we could afford a place near your brother, Tillie. The folks in Smithfield are doctors and lawyers, schoolteachers. I am proud of who we are, wife, but we don't have that kind of money. Even A. G. Gaston lives there, and he the richest colored man in Birmingham."

"Who's A. G. Gaston?" Georgia asked.

"We pass his motel every Sunday," Mama told my little sister. "Mr. Gaston also owns a funeral home, an insurance company, and other businesses here in Birmingham. His motel is the only place colored folks can stay when they come to town."

Then Mama looked at Georgia drinking her second glass of tea. "Don't drink no more tea, Georgia."

Mama didn't want to cause Georgia any shame, but I knew why she said that. Georgia hated going to the outhouse when it was dark, and she sometimes wet the bed.

The thought of a house with plumbing was real appealing. I would be some kind of happy to never worry about using the outhouse we shared with forty other folks on Bull Hill again. We did have a pee pot for when it was cold, but sometimes it would be so cold that my poor little sister would stay under the covers too long and accidently pee in the bed.

I thought about my little sister, so I put my two cents in about moving to Ivy Town. "Well, if Miss Boone says yes, when do you think we can move?"

"Real soon," Daddy Paul said. "I'm hoping for real soon."

4

Daddy Paul always kept his word, so the next day after church, we headed to Ivy Town.

"This place is so big," Georgia said as we arrived at Miss Boone's two-story mansion. The porch wrapped around the place like the white of an egg's yolk. I wondered what it would be like to live in a house that fine. The house, the fence, and the chairs and swing on the porch were all painted white, with two big stone lions set in the front yard. I had visited many white folks with Mama to deliver the clothes she made for them, but nothing that looked as grand as this.

"Paul, are you sure about this? Can't you see ain't no coloreds around here?" Mama said.

"It will be fine, Tillie. And I was told Miss Boone brought her colored maid with her here when she came from Boston. A woman named Maybell, who lives in one of the houses out back."

"What church does Maybell attend?" Mama asked.

"Don't know, but you can ask her yourself," Daddy Paul told Mama as he parked the car.

"Children, y'all coming too," he told us. "I want Miss Boone to see we are a good family."

Mama peeped in the rearview mirror to make sure her bun was straight as Daddy Paul rushed around the car to open her door. He took a bow and held his arm out like she was a queen.

Daddy Paul took us to the side door that looked like it might lead to the kitchen. Colored folks knew the rules around here. Do not go to the front door of a white person's house. Period!

I counted each step with my heartbeat. When Daddy Paul rang the doorbell, it sounded so loud it made me and Georgia jump.

"Good afternoon," someone shouted from the front door. We rushed back around to the front of the house to find an older white lady standing with the screen door cracked open just a little. "May I help you?"

"Good morning. My name is Paul Peele, and this here is my wife, Tillie. These are our children, Georgia and Rufus. If you are Miss Boone, we are here to speak with you."

"Yes . . . I am Frances Boone. Who are you again?"

Before Daddy Paul could tell her again, she cut him off.

"Tillie?" Miss Boone said, looking at Mama like she had just met a new friend. "I only heard the name Tillie once in Birmingham. You must be Rufus Jones's widow?"

"Yes, ma'am, Rufus was my husband. Those two children are his son and daughter. Paul is my new husband. We both work at your mill."

"I see," Miss Boone said as she opened the door an inch wider. "I see Ola at the market every Saturday morning. She said you make those fine clothes she wears?"

"Yes, madam. I make all of Ola's clothes. I love to sew, and folks seem pleased with my work."

"Tillie, you might be the answer to my prayers. Old age has taken all the meat off my bones. There is little need to buy new clothes when I got one foot in the grave and the other on a banana peel. Can you alter some of my dresses?" Miss Boone asked as the door opened wider and wider.

"I would be happy to alter your dresses, but today my husband, Paul, has other business in mind," Mama said.

"What kind of business?" Miss Boone asked.

"Well, we would make good neighbors if you would allow us to rent your house in the back. That's why we are here," Daddy Paul told her.

Miss Boone walked out onto the porch. Her face was filled with wrinkles and her hair was as white as her house. She had on a beautiful sky-blue dress that did look too big. The white flowers on the fabric matched her fine white pearls and earrings.

"I only have one empty house back there, and it's in terrible shape after the storm last year tore it to pieces. My son, Alex, said we should tear it down."

"Well, Miss Boone, I'm a good handyman. I can fix it up myself. It has to be better than where we live now. My wife and children get mighty cold in that shotgun house we rent from Mr. Hanks."

"Mr. Hanks!" Miss Boone chuckled. "You mean Smarty Hanks, the slumlord? That man is so tight-fisted, he'll never bother to fix the houses on Bull Hill." She looked at us with mercy. "I don't mind helping you, but I can't rent you that house—it needs more than a handyman. I am sorry."

I could not see Mama's face, but I could tell she was disappointed. She would never admit it because of her pride, but I knew she was tired of our house and all that came with it. Tired of hauling water from the well. Tired of sharing an outhouse with other families and having to pour bleach and scatter lavender into the toilet hole every day so it would not smell so bad. Tired of our wash freezing outside on the clothesline on the winter days when the sun didn't come out on Bull Hill. Yes, Mama was tired.

I looked at her arms as she was talking with Miss Boone. I could see the long dark scars that ran along her arms from stirring up the fire that heated our home. That made me cry. So many things had happened to my mama. I wanted Miss Boone to say yes so Mama would have a better house. So things would be a little easier for her. I crossed my fingers behind my back and made a wish. *Say yes, Miss Boone, please say yes.*

"Well, we thank you for your time, Miss Boone," Mama said. "Let me know when you have those dresses ready. I'll come over to get your measurements and pick them up."

Mama turned to walk away. Now I could see the disappointment on her face, and I guess Miss Boone saw it too, because she blurted out, "Wait! What about that house next door, Tillie?"

"What?" Mama swirled around like she was caught in a twister. She glanced over at the pretty white house that looked a little like Miss Boone's but smaller. "Oh, Lord, Miss Boone, we can't afford a house like that," Mama said.

"You don't know how much I am going to charge. Maybe we can work something out with all those dresses you'll be altering for me."

"We like to pay our own way, Miss Boone. We don't want anything for free," Daddy Paul said with his chest puffed out and not even two nickels to rub together in his pocket. I guess that was another one of the things I liked about him. He had his pride.

"Paul and Tillie, let's make a deal. You can rent the house for forty dollars a month if Tillie does all my sewing. Now, I didn't say *some*. I said *all* my sewing."

Mama looked at her new husband and smiled. "That sounds fine, doesn't it, Paul? You know how I love to sew, and it ain't a handout if I am working."

"Yes. Sounds fair enough," Daddy Paul said. "Thank you, Miss Boone. We're grateful."

"You are welcome. You can move in anytime after you square up your business with Smarty Hanks. Tell him you are moving compliments of Frances Boone," she said with a chuckle.

Georgia laughed too, and then the girl forgot all her

manners. "Miss Boone, does that house have a bathroom? I never lived in a house with a bathroom."

"Well, now you will—and you are going to have two bathrooms."

"*Two* bathrooms!" Georgia shouted. "No more outhouse!"

"Mind your manners, baby," Mama told her, but Miss Boone just laughed again. I think we all understood why Georgia was so happy.

"We sho' thank you, Miss Boone. I will come back in a day or two to square up our business, if that's all right with you," Daddy Paul said.

"Sounds good. I'll ask Maybell to find the key tomorrow. She's off Sundays. That way you can see the inside."

"Oh, thank you, Miss Boone. I'm sure the inside is fine. I will get your measurements and start your sewing as soon as we move in," Mama told her.

"Glad that is all settled, then. Now, you all have a nice Sunday." Miss Boone turned to walk away but stopped in her tracks.

"Tillie."

"Yes, Miss Boone?"

"I am sorry about your husband's insurance money. I will talk to my son. He lives in Boston, so the plant manager here handles matters like that. But I don't agree with the way he does business, and I keep telling Alex to find a new manager."

"I appreciate your kind words," Mama told our new landlady.

"I will see you soon. And please use my front door next time," Miss Boone said as she disappeared into her pretty house.

That was a happy Sunday, so Mama decided we should stop to get ice cream on the way home.

Daddy Paul had to use the back door of Joe's Ice Cream Parlor and pass by all the white folks waiting in front.

Seemed like every time he had to walk in a back door, Daddy Paul shrunk an inch. I watched him come out with our four cups of ice cream in a little brown container. His pride was melting just like our ice cream.

It made me angry to see Daddy Paul so hurt.

I was determined that I would march one day soon so that he'd never have to walk in a back door again.

5

"When we get to school, we need to talk with
YouOut. He got some information about the march,"
Slide said as we walked down the hill together to catch
the school bus.

"Lower your voice so the grown-ups don't hear," I
warned him as we got closer to the bottom of Bull Hill.
That's where all the schoolkids and some parents were
waiting.

Slide and YouOut were able to talk on the weekends
because they had phones in their house. Some of the
women who worked as maids had been given phones by
the white families they worked for. It was not a gift—it

was so that their bosses could call them in to work, day and night.

All the way to school, I didn't say a word to Slide about us moving. I figured my friends would be mad about me moving to a white neighborhood. I was kind of mad myself but was trying not to think about it, because other than having a bathroom and a nice home for Mama to live in, I'd rather be on Bull Hill with my friends and the folks who loved us.

"Come quick!" YouOut yelled when we stepped off the bus. He lived near school in the projects, so he always arrived early. The projects were cheap apartments mostly for colored folks, but they were better than living on Bull Hill, since they had running water and bathrooms. But Uncle Sam said they were just more segregation.

"So this is the deal," YouOut said. "My folks let Junie's friends come over all the time to play cards. But they're not playing cards. They're having a meeting of their own because they are going to join a bunch of the protests, and they have to get training."

"If they need the high school kids, they're going to need us too," said Slide. "I heard my mom talking last night, and she said her and her friends would be fired from their jobs if they marched. But guess what? We can't get fired because we don't have jobs."

"Exactly," YouOut said. "Our mamas may be scared, but we can't be scared. Junie says he'll tell me some of the stuff they're learning in nonviolent resistance training so that we can be prepared too. He says it's gonna happen soon."

We were all so excited at the thought of being part of the march that it was hard to concentrate on school the rest of the day.

⚜

Later that afternoon, Daddy Paul dropped Mama off at home and went to tell Mr. Hanks that we were moving. We could hardly wait for him to get home to hear what old man Hanks had to say.

When Daddy Paul finally walked in, he was dangling the keys to our new house. Georgia jumped up and down trying to grab them, and Daddy Paul lowered them so she could reach them. He smiled at my little sister, and she giggled as she held the keys and looked back at him.

"Mr. Hanks was mad as a hornet's nest when I told him we were moving," he said, taking the keys back from my sister.

"What did he say?" Mama asked.

"He said, 'You can leave anytime you want, but you ain't getting your twenty-dollar security deposit back.'"

"Never expected to anyway, knowing him," Mama said, and we all got a good laugh out of Mr. Hanks's foolishness.

"When are we leaving?" I asked.

"I told Miss Boone to expect us next Saturday. Ain't no need to stay around here for Hanks to try to start some mess," Daddy Paul said with pride.

"Then I have to get my toys packed right away!" Georgia said. She grabbed her doll and went off to start packing her stuff.

The next day after school, Mama put a box on the back porch for us to put old toys and outgrown clothes in. She said she was going to give it all to children who had less than we did, but I didn't know where she planned to find folks poorer than us.

"What y'all doing over there?" Slide shouted from his backyard as he practiced running from base to base in the homemade baseball field he set up.

"I might as well tell you, but just don't get mad, okay?"

"Don't worry, Rufus. I already know you're moving. Your mama told my mama. I was just waiting for you to tell me. Mama said y'all helping to integrate Ivy Town. Ain't nothing wrong with that, just like there ain't nothing wrong with us marching."

"Thanks, Slide. It ain't gonna be right not having you

next door. I don't even want to think about that . . ."

"Me neither. At least we still got school together," Slide said as he dropped his baseball and came over to help us pack.

"So what's it like in Ivy Town?" he asked.

"The houses are nice, but I think it's gonna be lonely without lots of kids around. If white kids live over there, you know they ain't going to play with us," I told him. "I just hope nobody bombs us."

"Bombs! Y'all better be careful. Promise me you will be careful, Rufus!"

I promised Slide I would be, but I have to say, thinking about bombs scared me.

After Slide went home for supper, the fear of the bombs left me because I was too busy feeling sad that we only had one week left on Bull Hill. Just one.

6

Even though Daddy Paul knew we weren't going to get our deposit back, he worked hard around the house to make sure we left that run-down place clean.

And before we knew it, it was the evening before moving day. We had one night left.

I was in the backyard helping Mama and Georgia take the clean clothes down from the line, where they'd been drying in the sun all day. Yesterday Mama had spent hours cleaning everything we had in the big black washtub.

"Here, Rufus. Put these outgrown overalls in the giveaway box. They'll be nice and clean for the next family," Mama said as she practiced her song for church on Sunday.

"*Still away, Lord, still away. I don't have long to say,*" she sang, and I joined in. Georgia stopped playing teacher with her dolls and tapped out the beat on the side of the washtub to give us a band. We filled Bull Hill with laughter until we heard someone knocking real hard on the front door.

"Who in the world is that?" Mama said. I looked through the back screen door and saw Daddy Paul opening the front door. It was Aunt Maggie.

"So, sister! Did you come to help us finish the laundry or to pack?" Mama asked. "Annie Ruth was supposed to help, but she ain't nowhere to be found. That just ain't like her."

"Right, sister! You need to help your big brother," Daddy Paul told her as he pinched her arm like they were still little kids.

"I can't help right now because I have to show y'all something. Please come with me," Aunt Maggie said.

"We still packing, we can't come now," Mama told her.

"Y'all come on. I will help you when we get back. It will take just a minute."

We followed Aunt Maggie farther down Bull Hill. When we got to her house, we saw every soul who lived on Bull Hill standing in her yard, waiting for us!

No wonder we couldn't find Slide and his mama, Miss Annie Ruth. They were holding a piece of cardboard with writing on it: WE WILL MISS YOU.

"Surprise!" Miss Annie Ruth said as Mama fell into her arms, and they both did some crying.

"Come on over here," Aunt Maggie told us as we looked at the big fire burning under the cast-iron pot. Mr. Lance, who lived two houses down from us, was frying up some fish.

"I thought I smelled fish," Daddy Paul said. Smelling fish on Bull Hill was not unusual. The menfolks caught fish almost every week, but nobody on Bull Hill had money for cornmeal every day, so fried catfish on Friday nights was a treat.

"You were so surprised!" Aunt Ola said, with a big smile on her face, as Mama hugged her and Uncle Sam.

"I love you, sister," my uncle told Mama.

"I love you too. I love y'all," Mama said, looking around at all our friends and at the pretty tables that the women had decorated with wildflowers in mason jars.

"Here, Tillie. I want you to have this quilt," our neighbor Miss Ida told Mama.

"Oh, Ida, I can't take this. You could get good money for this fine quilt, and you got children to feed," Mama said as she rubbed the quilt, which was made of every color in the rainbow.

"Take it. Our friendship don't have no price tag on it. Go on, now. Take it."

Mama cried some more as she hugged the quilt and Miss Ida.

One by one, our neighbors said their goodbyes to us while we ate and played music on Aunt Maggie's old record player.

All us kids were playing tag when Georgia came up to me and whispered in my ear, "I got to pee."

"Go ahead, girl," I told her.

She didn't say anything. She just stared at me. I looked at the sun going down and then the smile leaving Georgia's face. She was afraid of the dark.

"Come on, sister. I will walk with you."

Slide was listening and said he'd go with us too.

So Slide walked on one side of Georgia and I walked on the other as the sky began to get dark.

When Georgia was finished doing her business, we walked to the pump, where she washed her hands, and then we walked back down the hill together for the last time. Even though it was getting dark, I could still see the smile on Mama's face when see looked up Bull Hill and saw us coming toward her.

When it was time for everyone to go home, I felt like crying.

I was gonna miss Bull Hill and all the folks who lived on it.

Folks we loved.

Folks who loved us.

But I wasn't going to miss that stinking outhouse.

7

I woke up with the sun the next morning. I opened my window and threw a rock close to Slide's window to wake him up too.

"Rufus, it's too early for you to be waking folks up," Miss Annie Ruth yelled.

"Rufus Jr., you know better," Mama yelled back.

We didn't need a phone in those raggedy houses. Folks could just yell from house to house.

Slide put his head out the window. "Hey, I can't believe you leaving me today," he said with a sad face. "I think I'm going to miss you, boy."

"I *know* I'm gonna miss you." I laughed.

We leaned our bodies out our windows and shook hands.

Uncle Sam and Aunt Ola came to Bull Hill early in Uncle Sam's truck. Slide and his family helped us load Daddy Paul's car and Uncle Sam's truck with our belongings. Aunt Ola put all of Mama's dishes in her car because they said the men would surely break something.

When the house was empty, everyone stood around in the yard, and Mama had a real forlorn look on her face. Daddy Paul noticed everything about his bride, and he could feel her sadness.

"Go on back inside and say your goodbyes, wife. You lived here a lot of years. You got your own memories and heartbreaks here. You had good times too. I will wait for you in the car."

Mama climbed back up to the porch like she was walking her last mile. Georgia came over and took my hand. "Let's go too," she said.

We followed Mama up the steps and walked back inside to have a last look at the only home we'd ever known.

"Seems like we telling Daddy bye all over again, don't it, Mama?" I said.

"It do, son. It sho' do. But we ain't. He is always with us. He in our hearts, and his blood in your veins."

"Don't be sad, Mama," Georgia said, and we each hugged a side of her the way we did the day Daddy died.

"I'm fine. You gonna to be fine too. We had a lot of memories here, and now it's time to go make some more."

My heart hurt so bad as we stepped out of the house and I closed the door for the last time. The door that was the last link to our life with Daddy.

By the time we got back outside, our neighbors on Bull Hill had gathered in our yard. We hugged everybody one more time and got in Daddy Paul's car. Our Bull Hill family waved and cheered as we drove off. The children ran after us as we pulled off like we were in a parade.

"Bye!" Slide screamed like he was never going to see me again.

"Y'all enjoy them bathrooms," Miss Annie Ruth hollered.

I looked back at our old brown raggedy house. I could see the white sheets some of our neighbors had hung on their lines earlier that morning. The sheets were blowing against the wind like they were waving too as we drove away.

"Bye," we yelled until we could no longer see our friends.

Until we could no longer see Bull Hill.

8

When we turned into Miss Boone's driveway, she
was standing on the porch, waving at us like she was in a
parade too. I don't think a white person had ever lifted
their hand to wave at us before. We all waved back.

Before Daddy Paul could park the car in front of
our house, Miss Boone was off her porch and walking
across the yard. She was carrying a basket and handed it
to Mama as soon as she got out of the car. "Welcome,"
she said. "Maybell went to a bake sale at her church this
morning. She left you some muffins."

I could smell the muffins under a white-and-red
napkin.

"Thank you, Miss Boone," Mama said. "You and Miss Maybell didn't have to do that."

"We have manners. One is supposed to welcome a new neighbor."

Uncle Sam and Aunt Ola got out of his truck. "Morning, Frances," my uncle said as he started pulling furniture off the truck.

"How you doing, Frances?" Aunt Ola asked.

"Just fine. How are you all doing?"

I almost dropped the box that had GLASSWARE written on it when I heard them calling a white woman by her first name. No Miss or Mrs. . . . just Frances.

"I'll let you get settled in now. You all enjoy the house," Miss Boone said, and she turned and walked away.

Daddy Paul opened the door, and we watched Mama look at the pretty living room and followed her into the kitchen. She let out a shout of joy when she saw the new electric stove Miss Boone had put in. She ran over to the sink and turned the spigot to see our very own water run out. Then she looked in the little room off the kitchen, where there was a washing machine and a dryer.

"Lord, wife, why are you crying?" Daddy Paul asked.

"Because I am thirty-nine years old and I have never had a washer and a dryer. And I have cooked on a wood stove my whole life."

"Well, those days are over," Daddy Paul said as he picked Mama up and swung her around in our big new kitchen.

"Can we see the rest of house, Mama?" Georgia asked.

"Sure, baby girl." Mama smiled like a little girl herself as Daddy Paul let her down from her swing in the air. She looked so happy.

"Which room will I share with Georgia?" I asked Daddy Paul as he followed us down the hall.

"Share? You don't have to share, Rufus. The house has three bedrooms. So you two go pick your rooms before we start unloading. Just don't take the biggest room—that's for me and your mama."

"My own room!" Georgia ran down the little hallway and poked her head into each room. "I want this one!" she shouted as she ran into the smallest room.

"I don't mind if you take the bigger one," I told her.

"Thanks, Rufus, but I want this one. Look, the bathroom is right across the hall."

Being near the bathroom meant so much to her. No more long walks to the outhouse. No more holding it in on the nights it was too cold to get up. No more peeing in the bed.

We hugged each other. Then we began to unpack all the wooden milk crates and boxes full of our things.

We only stopped every now and then to visit our new bathroom and marvel at the running water and toilet.

Mama rushed around pulling out all her whatnots and placing them around the house. I watched her from the doorway of her bedroom as she laid her fine new quilt on her bed. Then she walked over to the window, and all there was to see were trees and sky.

"It sure is pretty here," she said, but all of a sudden she didn't sound so happy. I could tell she was missing the folks from Bull Hill. I missed them too.

"You okay, Mama?" I asked.

"I am fine, child," she said as she came over and wrapped her arms around me.

9

We worked all afternoon, and when it was dinner- time, Mama called us all into the kitchen.

Aunt Ola had set the table up for dinner all fancy, as if we were eating at the White House with the Kennedys.

"Let us pray," Daddy Paul said.

Before we could bow our heads, we heard loud voices arguing outside.

"What in the world is going on?" Uncle Sam asked as he and Daddy Paul rushed outside.

We followed them, leaving our smothered chicken behind.

It was Miss Boone having a showdown with a white

man. A tall colored lady was standing beside her like she was ready to take a bullet for Miss Boone. That had to be Miss Maybell. She wasn't saying anything, but she didn't look scared like Bull Hill women looked when white men came around.

"Miss Boone, you know this is a white neighborhood. We don't like no coloreds living here one bit," the man said as he looked down at Miss Boone, who was no more than five feet tall.

"We? Who are *we*? You don't even live around here. You couldn't afford a board in this neighborhood."

"Well, I work nearby, and folks are talking."

"Listen to me, young man. Folks are *always* talking. But they're not saying anything sensible. And in case you don't know it, this is my land! Everything from the woods to Boone's Creek belongs to me. These are my friends. Now go on home before I call the police."

"Call them. The sheriff knows I'm here," the man said. "I'm gonna leave now, but I'll be back. Coloreds ain't welcome here!" He spit some tobacco inches away from Daddy Paul's shoe. Uncle Sam grabbed Daddy Paul's arm to keep him from following the man to his beat-up old black truck.

"Trash ain't welcome here either!" Miss Boone shouted back. "And if you do come again, I will have my pistol waiting for you."

"Frances!" Miss Maybell said like she was shocked.

I was shocked too. Not only by the pistol, but by hearing Miss Boone's maid call her boss by her first name.

After the man had driven away, Daddy Paul said, "Now, Miss Boone, we don't want to cause no trouble."

"Trouble! The whole world's in trouble! But this is my land, and nobody is telling me what I can and can't do with it. Now y'all make yourself at home and have a good night," Miss Boone said. "Oh, and this is Maybell. If you need anything, let her know or let me know."

Miss Maybell said hello, and we all returned to our homes.

"What we going to do now?" Georgia asked as we all went back inside.

"Eat dinner," Uncle Sam said. He picked Georgia up and gave her a big hug.

We followed our uncle to the kitchen while Daddy Paul loaded the shotgun in his bedroom. I didn't see him, but I heard him.

I looked at my glass of iced tea. The ice had melted, like my excitement for our new house. It was hard to swallow dinner, but I did the best I could for Mama's and Aunt Ola's sake.

After dinner, we walked outside with Uncle Sam and Aunt Ola to say goodbye.

"Hmm. Looks like we forgot something," Uncle Sam said as he removed a big box from Aunt Ola's trunk.

We looked at the box and saw a picture of a television on it. "It's a housewarming gift," said Aunt Ola.

I guess a housewarming gift was different from a handout in Mama's eyes, because she seemed just as thrilled to receive it as me and Georgia. Just for a moment it made us forget about the white folks who hated us.

Later, when it was bedtime, Georgia peeked her head in my room. "That man said he'd be back, and I'm scared. You scared?"

"No . . . I am not scared," I lied to my sister. "But you can stay in here as long as you want."

"Thanks, but I'm a big girl, Rufus. I should sleep in my room."

"Okay, but let's leave our doors open. You can call my name real loud if you need me," I told her.

On Sunday morning, Mama announced that we could stay home from church to finish unpacking. It was a long day and nobody said anything about the man who threatened us the day before. Not one word.

We went to bed early, and I fell right asleep. But in

the middle of the night I was awakened by a noise in the backyard. I ran into the kitchen and peeked out the window to see Daddy Paul putting out a fire.

I ran outside in my pajamas. "What you doing, Daddy Paul?"

"Lower your voice, Rufus. Don't want to wake up Tillie and Georgia. This is a cross, child. They burned a cross in the yard."

Georgia was right. The mean man had returned.

I helped Daddy Paul cover the ashes with dirt.

"Daddy Paul, do you think moving here was a mistake? Maybe we should go back to Bull Hill."

I could only see his eyes, but I could feel his pain as he whispered to me. "There ain't no going back, Rufus. We just gonna have to be strong. It's going to be all right."

Daddy Paul sat on the grass and pulled me down with him.

"Listen to me real good. I am not your blood daddy, but I love you. It's my job to protect you. I also have to tell you the truth—and the truth is that the world is hard. Your life don't mean anything to some people, but it means everything to me and your mom and your family. And that's why we be going to all these meetings. We need to change things. I want you and the other children to live in a different kind of Birmingham than the one I was raised in. A free Birmingham."

Daddy Paul pulled me into his arms, and we looked up at the sky. It was so dark. Not even the stars wanted to shine on Birmingham that night. Then he hung his head and cried. I cried too.

10

The next morning on the way to school, Daddy Paul broke the news to Mama and Georgia about the cross.

"I can't believe we've been here less than forty-eight hours and they're burning crosses," Mama said.

"They trying to scare us and send a message to Miss Boone. But we staying. This is a good home for us to raise the children in. Besides, we got to show them that colored folks can live where they want to," Daddy Paul told Mama.

Georgia looked out the window and twisted her hair around her finger like she always did when she got nervous.

"Why do they hate us, Mama?" Georgia asked.

Mama said nothing.

"Did you hear Georgia, Mama?" I said. "She asked why white folks hate us."

"Let's go back to Bull Hill," Georgia said. "Everyone liked us there."

"No, children. We are staying. Miss Boone told us we are welcome, so we staying," Mama said as she eyed me in the rearview mirror.

"Well, they still hate us," I said as I eyed her back.

Daddy Paul spoke up. "Rufus, white folks have lived this way for so long, they can't get used to the changes that're coming. They think it's right to treat us this way. To be telling us where we can and can't go. But we ain't moving nowhere. Now, y'all do good in school today," he said as he pulled into the drop-off circle.

Mama blew us a kiss as we got out of the car. "I'm sorry we got to drop you off so early. Stay outside the school until the bell rings. It's going to be all right. We love y'all . . ."

"I love y'all too," I said as Georgia put her head through the car window and kissed Mama.

I could see YouOut walking toward us.

"Is it true?" he asked as my folks pulled off.

"Is what true?" I asked.

"Did you all buy a house in Ivy Town with all those

white people? That's what Slide told me at church yesterday—and where were you yesterday, anyway?"

"Well, we didn't come to church because we were unpacking," I said. "And we don't have no Ivy Town money. We're just renting a house from Miss Boone, who owns the steel mill. We're integrating Ivy Town because— remember what Miss Smith said? She said integration and marching are *both* important to the movement. So be quiet."

"Whatever you say, Rufus! But I sure rather be marching for change than having to live where you do. But anyway, take a look at this newspaper my mama got from her boss. It says right here that Dr. Martin Luther King Jr., Ralph Abernathy, and Dick Gregory are coming to town *this* week to bring more attention to the cause. They're going to have a meeting at 16th Street Baptist Church and then march down to City Hall. There are cutting through Kelly Park, and if we want to join them, we should go to the park."

I had been so busy packing and unpacking that I had not read the paper in a few days.

"Who is Dick Gregory?" Georgia asked.

"He's a comedian. Check him out on the news. He has been in out of Jackson, Mississippi, marching with Medgar Evers. Mr. Evers is just like Reverend Shuttlesworth. They are trying to get people registered to vote."

"I thought comedians just told jokes?" Georgia said.

"Not this comedian. I can't wait for him to come here," YouOut said with excitement.

"I can't wait for them all to get here—can't happen fast enough," I said. "We had a cross burned in our yard last night. Some welcome, huh?"

"Wait, what? They burned a cross in your yard?" YouOut said.

"Yes, so we are in for sure," I said.

"And I'm marching too," Georgia added.

I looked down at my little sister's innocent face. The thought of her marching scared me, but so did the thought of her not having her freedom.

⚜

Later that week, when Daddy Paul and Mama picked us up from school, Mama made an announcement.

"There's going to be a meeting at Uncle Sam's house after dinner, and Paul is going to go. With Dr. King coming back to Birmingham, there might be trouble. Folks here need a plan to keep him safe and keep us safe. You two don't tell a soul that Paul's going to meetings. We ain't on Bull Hill no more. It ain't safe to tell our business. That's including Maybell and definitely Miss Boone."

Mama still didn't trust Miss Boone, even though she stood up for us.

I couldn't believe that my uncle was holding a meeting at his own house. But I guess it made sense. Folks where he lived owned their homes, so they weren't as scared as we were. Folks back on Bull Hill knew they could be kicked out of their shotgun houses and fired from their jobs if their bosses found out they had been to any meetings.

When we got home, I changed clothes and put on my suit. Mama looked at me when I sat down at the table for dinner. "Son, why in the world do you have on your church clothes?"

"Because I'm going with Daddy Paul."

"Rufus Jr. . . . I told you no marching. That means no meetings either. I'm sorry, but you are just too young," Mama said.

"Go take your suit off," Daddy Paul said. He didn't raise his voice, but I could tell he meant business, so I got up and changed into my everyday clothes. I knew there was nothing I could say to change their minds, anyway. They wanted to protect me just like I wanted to protect Georgia.

Daddy Paul disappeared into the night as I watched from the window. I went to bed, but I tried to stay awake so that I could talk to him when he came back. It was no use—I couldn't keep my eyes open. I was too tired. Tired from getting up early and getting home late. Me and Georgia had to wait for our folks two hours every day after school. She was tired too.

I was asleep long before Daddy Paul came back, but I was the first to open my mouth at breakfast the next morning.

"What happened last night? Did you see Reverend Shuttlesworth?"

"Yes, I saw and heard Reverend Shuttlesworth," Daddy Paul said. "He is a brave man, but he has to be careful. They have already bombed his house. His life is on the line, but he keeps going. We all have to keep going."

"Bombed his house? When?"

"That was back in 1956 on Christmas Day, child. Dr. King says Reverend Shuttlesworth is one of the most courageous leaders we have."

"Wow, I guess nothing does stop him. So what's happening now? What did he say—is there going to be a big march?" I asked.

"Yes, I just don't know exactly when. There's going to be lots more of all kinds of protests—sit-ins and boycotts." Daddy Paul was about to tell me more, but Mama gave him the eye when Georgia joined us at the table, and that was all I got out of him that morning.

When we all arrived home from school and work

that evening, we could see Miss Boone waiting for us in our yard with her hands on her hips.

"Lord, what in the world is wrong now?" Daddy Paul said as we pulled up in our car.

"Good evening, Miss Boone," Mama said. "Is everything all right?"

"Evening, everyone. Everything is all right. Now, I have a suggestion . . . I don't want to get in your business, but I see you leaving with the children so early and coming back home with them so late. When do they study?"

"It ain't so bad, Miss Boone. They do their lessons, and they're both A students," Mama told her with pride. "But since we got to get to the mill by seven, we have to drop the children off at school early, and they wait for it to open. The colored children ain't allowed to ride the bus out here."

Miss Boone shook her head as she listened to Mama.

"We do get tired, Miss Boone, but we got to do what we got to do," Daddy Paul told her.

"Well, what time does school start?"

"Eight fifteen," Daddy Paul said.

"Eight fifteen! Well, I have a suggestion. I can drop them off at school on my way to the market. I go every day and have coffee with the ladies from my bridge club. So the children can ride with me."

"What?" Daddy Paul said, like he couldn't believe what he was hearing.

"Don't 'what' me, Paul. Have the children ready at seven forty-five Monday morning." She looked at me and Georgia. "And don't keep me waiting."

"Thank you for the offer, but we are fine," Mama said.

"Maybe you are, but I will enjoy driving the children to school. So, you get up Monday morning and go on about your business." Miss Boone quickly walked off before anyone could say another word.

"Mama, do we really have to ride with Miss Boone? We don't hardly know her," I said as soon as she was gone.

"And she's white," Georgia added.

"I don't like it either, wife. Miss Boone be putting herself and the children in danger," Daddy Paul said as we walked into the house.

"I will let Miss Boone know we will not be taking her up on her offer. I am planning to deliver some of her dresses in the morning. I will talk to her." Mama set her pocketbook and lunch bag down and looked at her baby girl. "Georgia, being white don't have nothing to do with Miss Boone's offer."

"White got something to do with everything," Daddy Paul mumbled.

"Husband, we ain't teaching hate in this house,"

Mama said as she washed her hands and got ready to fry some catfish. "I know we can find thousands of reasons to hate, but we got to teach the children better."

That was the end of that conversation as Mama instructed us to wash our hands so we could help.

"Rufus, get a half cup of lard out of the lard stand and put in the frying pan. Georgia, mix up the cornmeal with the salt and pepper."

Frying catfish on Friday night made me think about Bull Hill—seemed like folks there would die and go on to heaven if they didn't have their fish on Friday nights. It made me miss our neighbors and all of the things we used to do. But I was happy Mama still had us doing Bull Hill stuff.

So much had happened since we left Bull Hill, and it felt like there was something new to worry about every day. Now my worry was what would my friends think when they saw me ride to school with a white woman? Integrating Ivy Town was one thing. But riding to school with Miss Boone was another.

11

The minute Mama started gathering dresses to take to Miss Boone on Saturday morning, I jumped in to help.

"Can I go with you? I'll carry the dresses, Mama."

"Fine, but you stay out of grown folks' business when I'm talking to Miss Boone. Now open wide," Mama instructed me as she laid the dresses across my arms like we always did when I'd help her. Georgia ignored us and watched cartoons and filled the house with laughter.

I marched behind Mama like we were headed to war. Daddy Paul was working on his car out front, and he stuck his head out from under the hood long enough to say, "Good luck."

We knocked on the side door of Miss Boone's house for a while, but no one answered. Finally, Miss Boone yelled out the kitchen window, "I asked you to use my front door."

We walked around the house and climbed the front steps onto the porch of the pretty house.

It was my first time walking in the front door of a white person's house, and it felt a little funny.

Inside Miss Boone's house was so fine with everything you could imagine—pretty furniture, nice pictures on the wall, and china in the cabinets.

"Would you like some tea, Tillie? What about a brownie for you, Rufus? Maybell makes the best brownies in Birmingham."

Mama nodded that it was okay for me to have a brownie from the silver tray on the table. The tray was shining like everything else in the house.

"One is enough, Rufus," Mama said as my hands spread wide for two.

"Let me see the dresses while you drink your tea," Miss Boone said as she poured Mama a cup.

I almost choked on my brownie. I had been with Mama to many white folks' houses, but we never made it past the kitchen, much less to a living room. Mama might be invited to a bedroom to fix a hemline, but I was always told to wait in the kitchen. Nobody, I mean nobody, had ever offered my mama a drink of water, much less poured tea for her!

"Oh, you do fine work, Tillie. Mighty fine work," Miss Boone said as she turned the dress inside out and looked at the stitches. "You should have your own dress shop."

"Dress shop! Oh, Lord, I could never afford my own business. And right now I got to work at the mill to help Paul with the bills and feed the children."

"Never say never, Tillie," Miss Boone told her. "By the way, I spoke to Alex about the insurance money, and he's working on it. He wishes he had more time to get down here, but business keeps him in Boston. You know it was his daddy's idea to move to Birmingham. The mill was in my husband's family for two generations, and he wanted to be more hands-on in his semi-retirement. But sadly, he died a few months after we arrived here in 1960. He left the mill to me and Alex, so now we have to deal with it." Miss Boone fussed and fussed like her dead husband could hear her.

"I don't know much about those kinds of things. I just know what is right. I thank you for checking into the insurance money for us," Mama told her.

"You are welcome. I think I will try on one of my dresses now," Miss Boone said as she got up.

"Would you like us to wait in the kitchen?" Mama asked.

"You don't cook for me. Stay here and drink your tea."

Miss Maybell joined us in the sitting room. "Would you like anything else?" she asked.

"We're fine," Mama told her.

"Miss Maybell, why do you call Miss Boone by her first name?" I asked, and Mama tapped my knee to quiet me.

"I have worked for her since Alex was born, and years ago in Boston she asked me to stop calling her Miss Boone and always made Alex call me Miss Maybell. Miss Boone has her own idea about things, as you know. But it is harder down here."

"Where do you live?" I asked.

"Son, please stop asking questions," Mama told me.

"That's okay. He can ask. When the Boones moved here three years ago, my family came too. Mr. Boone offered my husband, Thomas, a job at the mill, and I stayed on as their maid. It was perfect for us because our children were grown. My boy, Miles, is a professor at Morehouse College, and my daughter, Sonia, is a professor at Spelman. Frances became a widow the same year we arrived, and my husband died last year. My children don't want me working anymore, but I am staying on a few more years for Frances—and also because I don't want my children paying my bills."

"Why didn't you move into the house we live in?" Mama said.

Oh, so she can ask questions, but I can't? I thought. *Grown-ups are really something else.*

"Frances offered it to me after my husband died, but I said no. Her neighbors don't want to see folks like us every day unless we cleaning their toilets or cooking their food. Don't nobody bother me back there. They know they wouldn't have a job at the mill if they bothered me."

"Lord have mercy, Maybell. I hope we didn't make a mistake by coming over here. I don't want no more trouble. They already burned a cross in the yard."

"Tillie, it will be all right. Like I said, people don't like to mess with Miss Boone, and you got a good man to look after y'all. I was scared to be there alone."

"Cross! Did you say someone burned a cross in your yard?" Miss Boone said as she came into the room with the dress on. She looked so nice.

"Yes, the second night we got here, someone burned a cross in the backyard. Paul put it out."

Miss Boone looked some kind of upset. "Listen to

me. You should have told me. If anything else happens over there, you let me know."

"I will, Miss Boone," Mama said.

"Yes, you will, and please call me Frances."

"I will try to remember," Mama said as she looked at the dress on Miss Boone. "That dress fits you real nice, Miss Boone—I mean Frances."

"Tillie, this dress fits perfect. I have lots more for you to alter." Miss Boone reached in the pocket of her pretty dress that was no longer too big and gave Mama a whole ten-dollar bill.

"Oh, no," my mama said. "We agreed that my sewing would cover our rent."

"Just take the money," Miss Boone insisted, putting the cash in Mama's hand. "And I'll be telling all the women in my bridge club about you. They use that mouthy Martha Pugh, and she can't sew worth a dime."

Mama said nothing as Miss Boone walked us to the door. Like me, she had never seen or heard of the likes of Miss Boone.

When we got outside, I pulled on Mama's dress a little.

"You forgot to tell Miss Boone that we aren't riding to school with her."

"I didn't forget, son! I didn't know how to tell her. So let's give it a chance—see how it works out."

"Okay, Mama. But why do you suppose she's so nice to us?" I asked.

"I don't know. Maybe they don't teach hate in Boston."

"You really think that, Mama?"

"I don't know for sure. I hope so. That's my prayer for people all over the world."

"Mama, if it ain't true, I hope it will be one day soon."

12

Mama and Daddy Paul had already left for work on Monday morning when Miss Boone drove into the yard, blowing her horn like she was in a fire truck.

"Good morning," she said with a smile as we climbed into the back seat. "No, no, no. I am not your chauffeur. Rufus, get in this front seat."

I did as I was told. I didn't know what to say. I had never been in a car with a white person before.

Smarty Hanks would let a bunch of us kids ride on the back of his truck when we worked in the fields for him, but not on the inside. Never! Stingy old man Hanks only paid us children a dollar a day for picking his cucumbers and chopping his cotton every summer.

"Cat got y'all's tongues this morning?" Miss Boone asked us.

"No, madam, it don't," we answered at the same time.

"I don't eat children, so it's okay to talk. Speaking of eating, Maybell made muffins this morning and saved some for you. You can put one in your lunch boxes."

I picked a muffin out of the basket next to me and passed one to Georgia. I opened my New York Yankees lunch box and put my muffin inside. I wanted a lunch box with Jackie Robinson on it, but there was no such thing in Birmingham.

"Thank you," we told Miss Boone as she pulled into the circle.

"You are welcome. I will be back at three fifteen," she said as we rushed out of the car.

I was hoping no one saw us, but no such luck— YouOut was standing outside waiting for me.

"What're you doing riding with that white lady?" he asked.

"That's Miss Boone. I told you we renting from her. She was coming this way, so she gave us a ride. Now mind your business."

"Right. Mind your business, because we ain't got

time for that," Slide said as he joined us. "Did you all hear that something like twenty people got arrested for trying to sit in the all-white sections of some drug-stores? Things are heating up now that Dr. King's here. My daddy said he'll be speaking on Wednesday night!"

"Yeah, and Junie told me they're trying to organize a march from 16th Street Baptist Church to City Hall. So all we have to do is be there waiting in Kelly Park. That way we can join in and follow them to City Hall."

"What about Bull Connor?" Georgia asked.

"Don't worry about Bull Connor. We all know he tried to stop Dr. King from coming to town, but it didn't work," Slide said.

"We still got to worry about him some, though," YouOut told us. "Junie says he's probably gonna bring in extra cops to keep us all from marching."

"Well, he ain't gonna stop us!" I said.

We talked and planned all day. Everybody had something to say about Dr. King coming to town. None of us wanted to be left out. We wanted our rights just like the white children. We were young, but we understood that Bull Connor was wrong. We understood that having to walk through back doors just to get ice cream was wrong. We wanted to be allowed to walk and live and get educated where we wanted. We wanted to be free.

"Afternoon," Miss Boone said when we got in the car to go home.

"Good afternoon, Miss Boone," I said. "Can I ask you a question?"

"Sure, Rufus, what is it?"

"I just wanted to know why you so nice and other white people hate us."

"*Hate* is a strong word, child, but I suppose it feels like that. It's ignorance. Some white people were taught that they are superior, and we know they're not. And some of them have hardly even had a real conversation with a colored person. They need to be woken up. The system is unfair. That's why so many of us are against segregation and we speak out."

"Miss Boone, do you think it's good that Dr. King and the other leaders are coming to help?" Georgia asked.

"Of course I do. Reverend Shuttlesworth has been trying to get equal rights for colored people a long time. He even tried to get a colored police officer on the force, but this town wasn't ready for that. I think Dr. King will bring national attention to this problem, and that's why Reverend Shuttlesworth has been asking him to come here for a while. We need Dr. King, but we need folks like your daddy and uncle too. I'm glad they are going to meetings and getting involved."

"How do you know they go to meetings?"

"Bull Connor goes out of his way to send a list with the names of everyone who is a part of the movement to white business owners and landlords. He assumes that all white people are on his side, but he's wrong."

"I see," I said. I was glad Miss Boone told us the truth because I was full of questions, and we talked more about the protests until we got home.

"Thank you for giving us a ride," Georgia said as we got out of the car.

"You are welcome. See you in the morning," Miss Boone told my little sister.

⚜

"Miss Boone ain't so bad. I like her, and she gave us muffins," Georgia announced to Mama that evening after Daddy Paul headed off to another meeting.

"Don't be begging," Mama fussed, but she looked surprised that we were not complaining about having to ride with her.

"We didn't beg, Mama," I assured her. "She offered us the muffins. Georgia is right—she's nice."

"Well, that is good. You all be nice to her. Everybody ain't prejudiced. And the Bible says to love your neighbor," Mama said.

"She knows a lot about Dr. King too. I asked her if she thinks children should march."

Mama looked at me. "Miss Boone ain't your mama. Me and Paul are responsible for both of you. Marching is for the grown folks and the college students. I better not catch you anywhere near a march. Do you hear me?"

"I hear you, Mama."

Mama reached out and held my chin in the palm of her hand.

"Look at me, son. I done buried your daddy. I ain't going to bury you too!"

Then she turned to Georgia. "You too quiet, so the same go for you!"

"But, Mama—" Georgia tried to say.

"But nothing! I am trying to keep you safe. I got to keep you alive. Now do your homework and go on to bed. I will clean the kitchen tonight."

We got up to leave, but I stopped at the door. "Don't you want us to have our freedom, Mama?"

She didn't even turn around to look at me.

"Mama, remember that Daddy always said to look people in the eyes when you want the truth. I just want to know. Don't you think fighting for our freedom is important? You keep talking about keeping us alive, but you never mention our freedom."

Mama turned around and looked me and then Georgia right in the eye.

"Don't you back-talk me, Rufus Jr. I want you to be free. I want you to be treated equally, more than almost anything. But I'm scared. You hear me? I'm scared for your life. I don't want you to end up like Emmett Till did down in Mississippi. There ain't a colored mother in the South that's not scared. Now go to sleep, you two."

Georgia and I did what Mama said and headed to our rooms. But Georgia stopped me on our way. "What's Mama talking about dying for? We just wanna march, right? We ain't gonna die."

"No, we ain't gonna die, Georgia. They're not gonna kill us, I promise."

Georgia seemed okay with my answer, but I wasn't so sure. Colored mothers were not the only ones scared. I was scared too.

13

"Good morning, Miss Boone—did you hear? Dr. King made it to Birmingham, just like he promised," I said before she could speak to us.

"I know, child. I heard he came early to keep safe," she said.

"Safe?"

"Yes—they often tell the press they are flying in on one flight and come on another. They get bomb threats all the time."

"Bombs!" my little sister said.

"Don't be scared, Georgia," I told her. "It's going to

be okay. That's why we're marching. So we *don't* have to be scared all the time."

"We? Did your parents say you could march?" Miss Boone asked me.

"No, ma'am, not yet they didn't. But I know I need to."

"Well, that is mighty noble of you," Miss Boone said.

"What does *noble* mean?" Georgia asked.

"It means to be honorable," Miss Boone told us. "To be willing to do things even when they are difficult."

I puffed my chest out and said, "I am noble, Miss Boone. I want to do what is right, and they are going to need us students." I looked over at my sister. "Georgia is noble too."

She smiled.

"I have another question."

"What is it, Rufus?"

"I want to know if you are going to let the plant manager fire my folks if they march."

She pulled into the drop-off circle and looked at me. "No, child! No one from the mill will be fired for marching. Not one person."

"Well, you are noble too, Miss Boone," I said as I got out of the car and we waved goodbye to her.

"Thank you, young man. I will see you both this

afternoon," Miss Boone said with a little laughter in her voice.

I wondered if all the folks at the mill knew their jobs were safe. This was good news because I know Daddy Paul wanted to march.

YouOut and a few students had already gathered in the shade of a tree, and YouOut was writing in his notebook.

"What are you writing?" Georgia asked when we got closer.

"I'm not writing! I'm drawing up the plans for us. Look! I made a map of the school. When we leave for Kelly Park, we can't use the school's front or back doors, or Principal Mack will see us. So we gotta use the side doors and maybe even the bathroom windows," YouOut said.

Slide got off the bus and came over right as the bell began to ring. That's another thing I didn't miss about Bull Hill—it was eighteen miles from school, and the bus was almost always late. Sometimes it felt like we were always behind everyone.

"Maps! Side doors! Windows! What in the world are we getting into?" Georgia asked as we walked into school.

"Whatever we have to," I said.

Still, all day long I thought about how much trouble

we could be in if we got caught. Not to mention disappointing Mama.

I decided I'd talk to Daddy Paul about what was going on, but he didn't come into the house after work. He dropped Mama off and kept on going.

Mama didn't say where he was, but I could guess, and I tried to wait up for him again, but Mama shooed me to bed.

⚜

"Did you see Dr. King?" I asked Daddy Paul before he even sipped his coffee at breakfast the next morning.

"I sure did."

"Well, what did he say?"

"Dr. King had lots to say. Part of Project C is boycotting white businesses downtown, so we're going to be working so that the shop owners feel the lack of business. That will hurt their wallets. And we're going to be bringing in more civil rights leaders for some mass demonstrations."

"Mass demonstrations. That sounds dangerous," Mama said.

"It's all dangerous, but it's necessary. With or without national leadership, colored folks are going to demand change in Birmingham. But we are going to continue practicing nonviolent resistance," Daddy Paul told us. "You know, it's been three years since the students at North Carolina A&T University had their sit-in at the downtown Woolworth's in Greensboro. It was time for Birmingham to give it a try—and wouldn't you know, lots of folks got arrested before they could even ask for a cup of coffee at Britt's lunch counter. Now a few other shops like Woolworth's, Pizitz, and Kress have temporarily closed to keep colored folks from even walking in the door."

"What in the world is going to happen to people who got arrested?" Mama asked.

"Reverend Shuttlesworth's working on raising money for bail. He knows that folks can't march if they can't afford bail or might lose their job."

I built up the nerve to say what I'd been dreaming about. "Daddy Paul, us kids really want to help. We don't have jobs to worry about either."

Mama didn't say anything. She looked at me with her *didn't I already explain all this to you?* eyes as she left the kitchen to finish getting ready for work. But at least she'd been letting me talk about it all with Daddy Paul. When Georgia followed Mama, I stayed in the kitchen because I had more questions.

"What else happened at the meeting?" I asked.

"What do you want to know, Rufus?" Daddy Paul

said as he poured me a half cup of coffee and topped it with milk. "Now, don't tell your mama. She don't think you old enough for coffee."

"Don't worry, I will keep this between us men. I want to know if there were children at the meeting."

He laughed when I said *us men*. I didn't tell him, but Daddy Paul was really growing on me. He was easy to talk to and he really cared.

"Okay, there's not much else to tell you," Daddy Paul said. "There were more high school students there—they seem to be coming from all over. And at the end of the meeting, we took up a collection. We're lucky to have celebrities like Harry Belafonte, Sidney Poitier, and Eartha Kitt donating thousands of dollars, but it's still not enough."

"Well, I hope we get more help soon, Daddy Paul. And what do you think about me going with you to a meeting? I think it's time! Don't you?"

"Let me talk to your mama," Daddy Paul said. "But she's right. It is getting dangerous out there. Bull Connor's men are everywhere, and they want to crush us. And now they're saying he's going to try to drain as much money out of the movement as he can by increasing the bail for the folks that have been arrested."

"Will there be more arrests?"

"Yes, this is only the beginning. There are still plenty

of people willing to protest, and so there will be more arrests. Now, it's getting late—go on and finish getting ready for school."

For the rest of the day, I couldn't get Bull Connor out of my mind. Why did he want to crush us? I went to bed scared that night. So scared I even dreamed that Bull Connor was chasing *me*!

14

I was still feeling scared thinking about ol' Bull Connor when Miss Boone picked us up for school on Friday morning.

"Miss Boone, why ain't you scared to drive us to school?" I asked.

"I never said I was not scared. Sometimes you just have to do things scared. So today, I am going over to the Tutwiler Hotel for lunch. I heard on the news that they are doing some protesting over there. I think it's time for this old lady to take a stand down here," she said.

"White people march too?" Georgia blurted out.

"Yes, child, white people march."

"What if they send you to jail?" I asked.

"Then I go to jail. If I don't pick you up this evening, get on the bus and go to Bull Hill. Your folks will pick you up."

"But how will they know? Who will tell Mama and Daddy Paul?" Georgia asked.

"Maybell will know what to do. Don't worry about us grown-ups, and don't worry about getting home from school. It will be all right. I promise."

Grown folks wanted to know everything about us, but they sure liked keeping their own secrets.

Miss Boone dropped us off and waved goodbye. I went straight to the kids who were in a circle talking.

"Daddy Paul said that Bull Connor putting more people in jail. That's where we might be going if we march."

"So be it. If grown folks going to jail, we can too," Angela said. Angela and her brother, Ace, lived in the projects near YouOut. Ace was on the football team, and he wasn't scared of nothing. Angela was not scared either. Or if she was, she didn't show it and was going to march scared anyway. Like Miss Boone said, sometimes we have to do things scared.

I worried about Miss Boone all day. I knew that

while we were plotting to join the march, she was already out there protesting.

When the bell rang, I hurried outside and looked down the line of the cars of folks picking up their children.

I ran down the sidewalk, holding Georgia's hand.

"Hey, Miss Boone," we said as we jumped in the car. "You made it back!"

"Yes, children, I made it back," she said in a soft voice.

"What's wrong, Miss Boone?" Georgia asked.

We could tell she had been crying.

She could barely get the words out. "Let's go home, children. Today is a day I will not forget."

"Why?" I asked.

"I went to the Tutwiler Hotel, and they arrested a few people. Women went to jail too. The police were dragging protesters out by their arms and legs. But they didn't touch me. They didn't arrest me."

"Because you white?" I said after mustering up the nerves.

"No, son, because my friend owns the hotel. And because I own the mill."

I told Mama and Daddy Paul about what happened to Miss Boone as soon as they got home.

"Well, don't be getting in her business. She knows what she's doing," Mama told me as Daddy Paul went off to another meeting. "And don't get out of that bed tonight, Rufus. Paul is tired when he gets home."

Oh my God! I thought. *Mama don't miss anything. I thought I was having secret man-to-man meetings with my stepdaddy!*

I went to bed with a load on my mind. I prayed Daddy Paul would get home safe. I would have to wait until breakfast time to ask him what went on in the meeting and who he saw. He had told me that Dr. King and Reverends Shuttlesworth and Abernathy were all visiting a bunch of different churches to drum up support since it was getting harder to convince folks to march. Folks weren't just worried about getting fired. Some landlords were threatening to kick tenants out of their houses if they marched.

I was also thinking about how to ask Miss Boone about the insurance money the mill owed us, because I figured we might need it if Daddy Paul got sent to jail.

So I sure had a lot on my mind, but somehow I guess I fell asleep.

The sound of Mama's pans banging in the kitchen wasn't the only thing that woke me up the next morning. It was Miss Maybell's screams that filled the early spring morning air. I ran outside in my pajamas. Everyone in the house followed me. Miss Maybell was standing in the yard looking at Miss Boone's pretty white house. It was covered with eggs and toilet paper.

Bad words were painted in black on the front porch. Miss Boone may not have been arrested for protesting, but people around here were mad and weren't going to let her forget it.

Miss Boone came outside and looked at the house. "Oh, Maybell, it's all right. A few eggs ain't going to bring the world to an end." She was calm like the sky after a bad summer storm. "Paul, would you please go in my house and call Sam? Ask him to send a few men from the mill to wash the house and paint it if they have to. I will make sure they get paid double today."

Still wearing her robe, she walked back on her porch. "What are you waiting for, Maybell? Let's go inside. We have to eat breakfast. And no eggs today, please."

"Wait," I said. "Ain't you going to call the police?"

"The police? Who do you think did this, Santa Claus?!"

I had to laugh a little at that, but Georgia just shook her head. "This is terrible!" she said. "Ain't you mad about your house?"

"No, I am not particularly mad. It's just a house. I am more concerned about what is going on in this city and all the folks stuck in jail who just wish they could go home to *their* houses."

15

After breakfast, we got into the car to go down-
town. We all needed new shoes. Mama made all of our
clothes, pants and skirts and shirts. The only things she
couldn't make was shoes and socks.

"We best hurry, Paul, or else all the shoes going to
be picked over. You know the white children and the
children from Smithfield all get new stuff for Easter,
and it's just a week away," Mama said as she rushed to
the car.

"Might not be that crowded," Daddy Paul said as
he opened the car door for Mama. "Colored folks are

boycotting most of the stores. We should be boycotting too."

"I know, Paul, but it's just for shoes. The children's Sunday shoes are way too small."

"Mama, I don't want new Sunday shoes," I said when we got near downtown.

"I *want* shoes, but shouldn't we be boycotting like they are doing on TV?" asked Georgia.

"Oh, my sweet girl, yes, we should be boycotting, but you can't wear shoes that're too small. That's all we're getting. Okay?"

"But they won't even let us try them on," I complained. "The ones we got last year never fit right and hurt my feet."

"And remember last year that lady wouldn't let you try on a hat, while all the white ladies were trying on lots of hats and shoes too!" Georgia reminded her.

"I know, babies. I am so sorry things are this way," Mama said as she glanced at us in the rearview mirror. She looked like she was about to cry, but she didn't.

A few minutes passed before Mama spoke up again. "Paul, please turn this car around. Let's go home. The children are right. We ain't going where we are not wanted."

"Sounds like a good idea to me. I'll find a place to turn around up ahead." Daddy Paul reached out and touched

Mama's arm. "Now, you all listen. We going home just like your mama said. But I want you to know that it will not always be this way. You children are young. When you're my age, you'll look back and understand what we are fighting for. Fighting so you can shop where you want to shop. Eat where you want . . ."

Before Daddy Paul could finish what he was trying to tell us, traffic slowed down and we noticed that a bunch of streets were blocked off. Police were everywhere. We could see a group of people marching in front of 16th Street Baptist Church.

I could see DJ Shelley Stewart standing in the window of the radio station, watching just like we were.

"Georgia, look! It's DJ Shelley."

"Really? Yes! It *is* DJ Shelley! It's him," Georgia squealed.

Everybody in Birmingham listened to DJ Shelley—even Mama when she wasn't listening to her gospel music. DJ Shelley might be colored, but the white children liked him as much as we did. All the children in Birmingham liked to stand at his window whenever they went downtown. He was usually smiling and making us happy. Not today!

"Husband, did you know they were marching today?" Mama asked as I looked at DJ Shelley.

"Yes, but I didn't plan to come this way. Reverend

Shuttlesworth is marching today, and your brother's with them. This is just the beginning. Dr. King's brother, the Reverend A. D. King, is also marching from St. Paul Methodist all the way downtown tomorrow."

"Marching tomorrow? They marching on Palm Sunday?" Mama asked.

"That's right. We're not letting up now. It's time to keep the pressure on."

"Why are they marching in their church clothes?" Georgia asked.

"They're sending a message, child. They want white people to see how dignified we are. They paint us to the world like we are animals, but when the reporters come, they will see the truth. We are the peaceful ones."

"Mama, it's Reverend Shuttlesworth," I interrupted, pointing.

"Yes, it sure is," Mama said, and we watched as the police approached him. When the police got closer to the protesters, some of the men and women walked away from the march. DJ Shelley walked out of his studio and looked on from the top of his building's steps.

"Where are the other people going? Why are they leaving him?" I asked.

"That's what they've been taught to do when a bunch of leaders are together. A few will always leave to make sure they're not in jail at the same time."

Daddy Paul stopped talking and began to drive faster. "We better get out of here, wife. Me and Sam can't be in jail at the same time."

As we pulled away, we saw the police arrest Reverend Shuttlesworth.

"I hope Uncle Sam's okay," Georgia said.

"Me too, child. I hope so too," Daddy Paul said. He tried to turn the car around on a side street, but a police officer waved his hand to stop us. Daddy Paul stopped the car and rolled down the window.

"This is as far as you can go, boy. Folks like you causing too much trouble today. Ain't nobody else allowed in the Kelly Park area!"

"Boy?" Daddy Paul said as the muscles throbbed in his neck.

Daddy Paul put his hand on the door handle.

The white cop put his hand on his pistol.

"Please, Officer. We don't want no trouble! Paul, let's just go home," Mama said.

"You best listen to her, boy. Go on home now. Take your gal and her children with you."

He said that like Mama was not his wife and we didn't have a daddy. I wanted him to know we had two daddies.

"That's my mama and stepdaddy," I said.

The officer leaned over in the car.

"What did you say?"

"Nothing, Officer. He was talking to his sister," Mama said. "We are leaving now. Let's go, Paul, please!"

Daddy Paul pulled off.

"Rufus, what were you thinking?" Mama said. "You can't be talking back to the police. They have guns and they will use them on colored boys like you. Do you understand?"

"Yes, ma'am."

Daddy Paul said nothing the rest of the way home, and when he got out of the car, he stood beside it like he was trying to steady himself to walk to the porch.

"Aren't you coming in, honey?" Mama asked.

"I need a minute," he told her. "I'll be in shortly."

I put my hand on the doorknob to go back outside with him.

"Stay inside, Rufus. Sometimes a man needs time alone. Paul will be all right," Mama said. But she kept peeking through the screen door to check on him. She knew he was not all right.

Then he just sat on that porch rocking like he used to when he was waiting for Mama to love him. Waiting for her to marry him.

I am so glad she said yes.

Uncle Sam finally drove up around dinnertime, and Mama went on the porch and hugged him real tight. We followed her outside and hugged our uncle too.

"Brother, I am so glad to see you. I thought you were in jail," Mama told Uncle Sam.

"They didn't arrest me this time, but it won't be long. They arrested a big crowd of folks today," Uncle Sam said.

"I will march the next time, Sam," Daddy Paul said without even looking up. Then he explained to my uncle what happened with the police. I thought he was going to scream as his voice got louder and louder. Georgia rubbed his arms, hoping to calm him down.

"I'm all right, baby girl," Daddy Paul said, and he took a deep breath.

"I know this is hard. It's hard on all of us. But, brother, it'll be best if you stay put for now," Uncle Sam said. "The people in Smithfield will look out for Ola. There is no one over here to look out for your wife and children if you go to jail."

"I hear you, I hear you. Okay—for now," Daddy Paul said, but I'm not sure he really agreed.

"Lord have mercy. Y'all be careful!" Mama said.

"What happened to Reverend Shuttlesworth?" Daddy Paul asked.

"Now, you know we don't have to worry about Reverend Shuttlesworth. There ain't a white man in Birmingham that he's afraid of. Don't forget all the times they tried to kill him and failed," Uncle Sam said.

"They did?" Georgia's eyes grew big.

"Yes," I said. "YouOut told me that one Christmas night they bombed Reverend Shuttlesworth's house, and him and his bed went flying up in the air like it was a magic carpet ride!"

"That's right," Uncle Sam said. "And Reverend Shuttlesworth said he knew it was God that saved him and his family."

"Are they going to bomb our house too?" Georgia asked.

"No, baby," Mama said as she pulled Georgia close and hugged her. She didn't even fuss about me putting my nose in grown-up business.

"Why didn't Reverend Shuttlesworth stop after getting his house bombed? Isn't he scared?" Georgia asked.

"Scared! No, baby, he is not scared. The next year, he tried to enroll his children in an all-white school. The cops met him at the door and beat him with bicycle chains and brass knuckles. I have never known a man like Shuttlesworth. He is relentless," Uncle Sam said with pride.

He turned to Daddy Paul and passed him an envelope. "Paul, hide this money in the house. If I go to jail, you bail me out. Don't have Ola coming down to the courthouse." Then he turned to Mama. "Sister, if Paul ends up in jail, you use the money to bail him out. Always get one of the men from church to meet you downtown if you can't reach me."

"Brother, you know how we feel about handouts," Mama said. Uncle Sam and Daddy Paul looked at her like she had two heads.

"Little sister . . . pride is one thing, being stubborn is another. Reverend Shuttlesworth is in jail. Dr. King's brother is going to be marching downtown tomorrow. He will probably go to jail too. Your husband almost got his head cracked today. We at war! You hear me? This is a war!"

16

"Let's get moving, children. 16th Street Baptist is going to be full of folks today. You know what it's like on Palm Sunday," Mama said, in between singing "Walk with Me, Lord."

Every now and then she would get to shouting. *"Thank you, Lord! Thank you! Thank you for your mercy. You keep us safe from all hurt, harm, and danger! I just want to thank you! Hallelujah."*

"Sing, wife, sing!" Daddy Paul shouted from the bedroom as he finished getting dressed. Georgia was in her room getting dressed and serving as backup singer for

Mama. Her voice was good, but nobody in Birmingham could outsing Tillie Jones Peele.

I was dressed and sitting in front of the television, hoping we could get news about all the people that were in jail.

Daddy Paul came in the room and stood over me to see what was happening too.

"Stand up, Rufus. Let me fix your tie."

I stood up and faced my stepdaddy, and he looked at me with so much sadness as he straightened my tie like Daddy used to do.

"Daddy Paul!"

"Yes, son?"

"I am glad you married Mama."

"Thank you, Rufus! I am glad I married her too. I am glad I have you and Georgia. Now let's get to church."

"You look pretty, little sister," Paul told Georgia as we all walked to the car. "You and your mama just plain pretty."

Georgia smiled and spun around in her dress.

When we got to the 16th Street Baptist Church, word spread quickly that Reverend A. D. King was just blocks away, getting ready to lead the march to City Hall. Some of the 16th Street members were going to join them.

I cut my eyes at YouOut and saw that his mama, Miss Pearl, was watching him like a hawk. But while she was watching YouOut, Junie slipped through the side door.

Mama locked eyes on me from the chorus stand. I read her lips: *Don't move.*

Reverend Cross preached a good sermon, but I don't think too many people heard it, with their minds set on marching to City Hall.

After the service, we walked outside onto the steps and could see crowds forming across the street into Kelly Park.

"What is that?" Georgia asked as she moved closer to me.

We all looked at the big tanker truck sitting in Kelly Park. The kind you see in the movies.

"What in the world?" YouOut said as Bull Connor stepped out from behind the tanker with more policemen. Police with big German shepherd dogs.

The dogs started barking, but people kept on walking into Kelly Park, and we spotted Junie and some other teenagers in the front of the crowd.

"STOP!" Mama and all the women yelled as the dogs barked at Junie and his friends.

The police gave the dogs enough room on their leashes to almost reach the teens, which forced Junie and his friends to back up, but they refused to leave the park.

Daddy Paul started walking away from us toward the park as the dogs ran toward the teenagers.

Mama yelled his name, and he turned around for a minute to say, "It's all right, wife. I'll be all right. Go on home with the children."

I guess his deal with Uncle Sam was off. Daddy Paul was marching now! We could no longer see Daddy Paul as Uncle Sam held Mama back.

"Go home with the children now, Tillie. Ola will drive you, and I'll be there shortly," Uncle Sam said as he walked us to the car. After we were safe inside, he walked back to the church.

Nobody talked much on the way home, and as we were getting out of the car, we ran into Miss Maybell, who was coming home from her church too.

She stopped in our yard and started talking real fast. "They had dogs today! Dogs waiting for Reverend King and the others right outside our church! The police used the dogs so nobody could make it to City Hall."

"There were dogs in Kelly Park too," Mama said. "The police looked like they were getting ready to set them on some teenagers. I hope those teens are okay! I don't know what happened to Paul either. He joined the march."

"Lord have mercy. I will be praying," Miss Maybell said as she rushed over to Miss Boone's house.

I could not believe what was happening. Dogs and tankers at church. It sure felt like we were at war!

I heard Mama in the kitchen praying for everyone's safety while she was setting the table. Before I had a chance to turn on the news, Uncle Sam was at the door with Aunt Ola.

Mama rushed over and let her brother in. "Where's Paul?"

"I'm sorry, sister, but he has been arrested."

"Oh God!" Mama cried as Aunt Ola tried to comfort her.

Uncle Sam sat down like he was out of air, and I got him a glass of water.

We all waited for him to drink his water. It felt like a whole hour passed.

"Paul and a few members from our church are in jail. I'll bail him out in the morning."

"Let me get the money you gave me," Mama told my uncle.

"No, you keep it. You might need it later. I have enough right here in my pocket."

Mama calmed down just a little knowing Uncle Sam had the bail money and she had more under the bed mattress.

"What about Junie and the other teenagers? Are they okay?" I asked.

"Junie is okay, but his friend Leroy Allen was bit by one of Bull Connor's dogs. He was taken to the hospital."

"I can't believe they let the dogs bite the children!" Aunt Ola said with horror on her face.

"I know. It was one of the worse things I've ever seen. We couldn't believe it either."

"What's going to happen, Uncle Sam?" Georgia asked.

"We don't know what will happen next. But I think the eyes of the world are going to be on Birmingham. We are going to make change happen, but a price will be paid."

Uncle Sam stood up and looked at all of us at the table.

"Sister, I will let Frances know I am going to be late for work tomorrow. She can let the plant manager know. You take the day off and meet me at the jail at nine sharp. Children, go on to school tomorrow. We cannot fold because Paul is in jail."

Uncle Sam and Aunt Ola stopped by Miss Boone's house, and then they went on home.

The house was sad and empty without Daddy Paul. Sad and empty like it was the night we went to bed without my blood daddy.

"Lord, have mercy! Keep my husband safe. Keep them safe," Mama prayed.

"You want to sing, Mama?" Georgia asked. "I know it makes you feel better."

"It does, baby, but not now. Not now. Y'all go on to bed, please."

I guess all the songs were gone from Mama's heart that night.

17

"Miss Boone, do you think they'll let Daddy Paul out of jail?" I asked the next morning.

"I do! Your uncle Sam will be able to bail him out today. I just don't know about the other people who were arrested. Most folks don't have bail money. I'm making a donation to help."

When we arrived at school, all the children were talking about Bull Connor's tanker and the dogs. Everyone was mad that the dog was allowed to bite Leroy.

"Junie said Leroy is doing okay," YouOut told us as we huddled in front of the school. "And they ain't gonna let the dogs stop them."

"My stepdaddy is in jail," I told everyone.

"My daddy went to jail too," another kid said, and more chimed in.

"Mine too—and his boss at the cleaners sent his maid to tell us he's fired."

I listened to all my friends tell their stories. Either their folks were in jail, scared to go to jail, or scared to lose their job.

"Y'all sit tight," YouOut said. "Junie's friends coming over tonight. I will listen in to see what's happening next. When they march, we march, right?"

"Yes!" we all agreed. We were angry and we were ready.

We went to class, but it was hard to focus with Daddy Paul locked away in Bull Connor's jail.

Georgia and I were happy to see Miss Boone when we got out of school. We couldn't wait to get home to see if Daddy Paul was there yet.

My heart was racing as we turned onto Ivy Town Lane.

Georgia spotted Daddy first. "He's home!" she shouted.

And there he was, sitting with Mama on the porch.

We jumped out of the car and ran up to him and gave him the biggest hugs ever.

Miss Boone got out of the car and joined us. "Afternoon, everyone. I am so glad to see you are home, Paul."

"Thank you! I am glad to be home."

"Here, Tillie, I have something that belongs to you." Miss Boone gave Mama an envelope.

"What is this?" Mama asked as she opened the envelope. "What in the world?!"

I peeped over Mama's arm and looked at the paper. It was a check with more zeros than I had ever seen in my life.

"This is the insurance money that's owed to you," Miss Boone said. "I hope it will help."

"Help? This is enough money to last us the rest of our lives. Enough for the children to go to college."

That is when I saw something I thought I would never see.

Miss Boone reached out and hugged Mama. Mama didn't know what to do. She wrapped her arms around Miss Boone like she was touching a hot stove.

"God bless and keep you always. We are grateful!" Mama said as the two women cried together.

"You are welcome. I'm sorry it took so long to get it to you," Miss Boone told Mama. Then she said goodbye and went home.

"I am happy for you, wife. Happy for the children," Daddy Paul said as we went inside.

"Husband, this will help us all. We are a family."

"What are we going to do with all that money, Mama?" Georgia asked.

"I am going to help Paul buy us a house. And besides college, I'm going to save this money for a rainy day."

"Rainy day! Ain't every day a rainy one when you poor?" I said.

That just tickled Mama and Daddy Paul too.

"Don't worry, we can buy a few things that we need. And you can both get a few things you want. Okay?" Mama said as she looked at the check again.

"Can we order some shoes from Sears so we don't have to go downtown anymore?" I asked Mama.

"Yes, you can order shoes, and winter boots too," Mama said with a big smile.

"I know what I want," Georgia said as she looked down at her white dolls in her make-believe school. "I want some colored dolls to add to my classroom."

"Well, we will see what's in the Sears catalog this year," Mama said, but I could tell she knew good and well she wasn't going to find any colored dolls for Georgia in any catalog.

Daddy Paul smiled as we told them all the things we wanted. Even if he might not want to use my daddy's money, he wanted us to be happy. If we were happy . . . he was happy.

"Can we go to Kiddieland?" Georgia asked. "I want to ride the Ferris wheel. You said before we couldn't go 'cause we didn't have the money. You have money now."

"I sure wish you could go to Kiddieland, Georgia. But I'm afraid the answer is still no."

"But why, Mama?"

"Because colored children aren't allowed to go to Kiddieland," Mama said. "I said it was because we didn't have money and told a little lie because I was trying to protect you."

"But, Mama, you *never* lie," Georgia said, like the world was coming to an end.

Well, she did kind of lie when she used to tell us to tell Daddy Paul that she was not home. But I suppose she had her reasons.

Mama was looking down at Georgia's sad little face. "I know. I'm sorry. You see, colored children are not allowed there, and no amount of money will change that. Not now, anyway. But I promise you, folks in Birmingham are doing everything they can to change that."

"I forgive you, Mama. I know you were trying to protect us, but you can't. And I don't even want to go to Kiddieland anymore." Georgia looked at the check sadly, realizing it could not buy our freedom.

18

We were all happy that Daddy Paul was out of jail.
Mama and Georgia sang real loud while they set the
table for dinner, and I was glad God put a new song in
Mama's heart.

We were even happier and jumped for joy when DJ
Shelley announced that Reverend Shuttlesworth had
been released from jail too.

After dinner, Mama and Daddy Paul discussed the
insurance money and the big decisions they were making. "I'm not quitting my job yet, Paul," Mama said.
"Let's stay here awhile and do what we came here to do.
We going to integrate Ivy Town, and then we'll move on

to a house of our own."

She reached across the table, held Daddy Paul's hand, and then looked at us. "I am going with Paul tonight. It's going to be an important meeting over at 16th Street Baptist."

"Why now, Mama?" Georgia asked.

"Well, Georgia, that's a good question. I've decided this movement needs all of us. Paul went to jail for peacefully protesting against the police letting a dog bite a child. That could have been you or Rufus. It could have been Slide or YouOut or any of your friends from church or school. I can't sit home while children are being bitten by dogs."

"Mama, we want to go to the rally too. Right, Rufus?" Georgia said as she elbowed me in the side.

"Yes! We do. Mama, you're right that the movement needs all of us, so we want to go. We *need* to go!"

"Let's take them with us," Daddy Paul said. "We know we can't shield them from what's going on."

"All right. Get your sweaters. It gets cool in the church at night," Mama said. We were so surprised she agreed, that me and Georgia were at the door with our sweaters before Mama was up from the table.

When we got to the church, cars were on every corner and the parking lot was full.

"Sit back here, children. Don't leave, not even to go

to the bathroom," Daddy Paul said when we got inside the church.

I knew Dr. King was still in town but didn't know if he was coming to 16th Street Baptist. He was still going from church to church, encouraging people to join the protest. But when I looked out the side door, there he was, Dr. Martin Luther King Jr.

Everyone stood up and clapped, but Dr. King was not there for cheers. He was there for our freedom.

Everybody listened to Dr. King and seemed to agree with everything he said. But I was surprised that the one thing he couldn't do was get people to stand as volunteers for the next march. People were afraid. As I looked around, only a handful of adults stood up.

Then I saw Junie stand up, and more teenagers joined him, until just about every student was standing. I moved my legs to stand, but Mama pulled me back down.

Dr. King prayed for a little while, and then he told us he had come to Birmingham to help even if it meant going to jail. That nothing was going to stop our movement. He said the eyes of the world were on us. He said we could not be stopped.

Hearing Dr. King gave me hope. Hope that things in Birmingham really could change. That what Daddy Paul said was right. That the world *would* be different when me and Georgia were grown.

19

When we got to school the next day, I ran over to my friends to tell them what I heard at the rally, but YouOut was already telling everyone. He was at the rally too, but there'd been so many people there, we didn't get a chance to talk.

"Okay, Junie said they're waiting to hear exactly when the big march will be. He said students from a bunch of colleges are going to come when they get the word," YouOut said.

YouOut had become our leader in a way, just like Reverend Shuttlesworth was leading the grown folks. No one told YouOut he was the leader; it just happened because he was good at remembering stuff and answering questions. Also, he didn't seem scared of anything.

"So Junie wanted me to tell you all that the main thing we have to remember is this—we have to stay nonviolent when we march," YouOut said. "No throwing rocks, no fighting. We can't use any bad words. And it's not easy to stay nonviolent when there's dogs and stuff attacking you."

"Yeah," Angela said. "My cousin said the best thing to do when the cops come at us is to stick together and sing."

"Well, good thing we all like to sing," YouOut said, and then Georgia burst out in song, just like our mama would do.

"*Woke up this morning with my mind stayed on freedom . . .*"

Soon my little sister got everyone singing.

Georgia knew even if she wasn't allowed to march, she could still use her voice to protest and to help the cause. She made us all feel better.

The week went by in slow motion as we waited for YouOut to bring us more information from Junie each day. I watched television and listened to the radio to see what

I could find out. We asked Miss Boone questions as we rode to and from school, and one afternoon she told us, "There's an injunction against Dr. King and other all protesters in the city of Birmingham."

"What's an injunction?" Georgia asked.

"It's an order saying they don't have permission to march. It means if they do, they are breaking the law," Miss Boone told her. "It means the city leaders are scared and trying to stop this movement in its tracks."

"Do you think it will stop Dr. King and Reverend Shuttlesworth?" I asked.

"I don't believe so. Not much stops them," Miss Boone said as we got out of the car.

The next day was Good Friday, and I was kind of mad because that meant no school and no catching up with my friends about the latest news. It also meant the mill was closed and all the grown folks were home.

Mama had a long list of chores for me and another list for Georgia.

"Mama, can we hire a maid with some of the insurance money?" Georgia asked as she cleaned the bathroom.

"Child, no!" Mama laughed.

The one chore I liked was delivering the clothes Mama altered to Miss Boone, since I never got tired of talking to her.

"Come in, child, and sit down. Watch television

with me," Miss Boone said as Miss Maybell came out of the kitchen and poured me some iced tea.

"Rufus, don't you visit too long," Miss Maybell said. "It's time for Frances to eat her lunch."

"Stop fussing, Maybell. Come on over here and join us."

Miss Boone leaned forward in her chair and changed the channel as Miss Maybell pulled up a chair. The reporter was talking about Dr. King being in Birmingham and Medgar Evers being in Jackson, Mississippi, and both of them stirring up "trouble."

"Do you know who Medgar Evers is?" Miss Boone asked when we heard the reporter say his name.

"Yes, madam, I sure do! I want to be a sportswriter one day, but I want to write about the movement too, so I read everything I can. I read all about Medgar Evers in *Jet* magazine, and our teacher told us about him. He is the president of the Mississippi NAACP, and he got the university there integrated. Now he's trying to get people registered to vote down in Jackson."

"Very good, Rufus. I'm glad your teacher is telling you about leaders like Medgar Evers—all students should know about him and his work."

Miss Maybell just sat there and listened to me talk to Miss Boone. She was so tickled that I knew all about Mr. Evers, she gave me an extra cookie and one for Georgia.

"Thank you, Miss Maybell," I said as Miss Boone waved her hand for us to stop talking and watch the television.

On it we could see Dr. King, Reverend Shuttlesworth, and Reverend Abernathy being led across the street by the police.

"Oh no! They're arresting Dr. King! They got Reverend Shuttlesworth and Reverend Abernathy too. Bye, Miss Boone! Bye, Miss Maybell! I have to go tell my folks," I said as I rushed out the door.

As I ran toward the house, I shouted, "Mama! Turn on the TV. They just arrested Dr. King. They arrested all of them." Daddy Paul stopped washing his car and followed me inside.

We all gathered around the television and watched as the paddy wagon drove off.

"They took Dr. King. Does that mean the movement is over?" Georgia asked, with tears in her eyes.

Mama pulled her close and spoke with determination. "No, child. The movement's not over. This movement will only be over when you have the same rights as the little white girls in Ivy Town. It is definitely *not* over."

20

Colored folks and good white folks like Miss Boone were some kind of upset that Dr. King was in jail on Easter Sunday. The days that followed were filled with fear as small groups of people continued to protest for the release of Dr. King.

Daddy Paul went to meetings every night. He wouldn't let us go. Every night I waited for him to come home, and Mama didn't fuss about me waiting anymore. Her courage had started to outweigh her fears. She wanted freedom for her children.

Some nights Mama would wait up for Daddy Paul too. She had the same questions I had.

When would Dr. King be released?

What would happen next?

It felt like our leaders would be staying in jail for a while as the days turned into a week. But one evening I was in the kitchen helping Mama snap some peas for Sunday dinner when Georgia yelled to us from the living room, where she was watching television. "They are out! Dr. King is out of jail!"

We all ran to the television just in time to see him walk outside. It was good knowing that Dr. King getting free was probably on every television station that evening.

"Praise the Lord!" Mama said. "Praise the Lord!"

YouOut was talking a mile a minute when we met near the circle on Monday morning.

"Listen, Junie said the big march is coming soon. The grown-ups are taking too long or are too worried, so the kids have to step in. We have to make sure we listen to DJ Shelley every day. He's gonna give us all a secret code for when it's happening."

"How will we know what DJ Shelley is talking about if it's in code?" Slide asked.

"We already know the big march is set for May

second. Junie said that's the date. Just read between the lines. If he says it's time to rock and roll or that there's a party going on, it means go to the park," You-Out told us. "D-Day is coming soon."

"What's D-Day mean?" asked Georgia.

"In war, it's what they call the days of big battles," Angela told her. "Our D-Day is coming."

"Dang gone right," YouOut said.

I looked at everyone in our circle and said, "We all know this isn't a game. Junie's friend got hurt. That could happen to us."

YouOut spoke up. "It could, but we're ready, so be it!"

"Yep. We are ready to claim our freedom," said Georgia, and she broke into song with her real pretty voice. *"Freedom, oh, freedom. Oh, freedom over me."*

Everybody started singing along with my sister, and I couldn't have been prouder of her.

21

DJ Shelley's voice on the radio filled the kitchen.
"Good morning, Birmingham! Today is a great day! It's time to rock and roll in the park. Bring your lunch and your toothbrush, because we are going to be there all day."

"Georgia!" I shouted. "Did you hear that?"

Georgia was standing in the doorway.

She started jumping up and down, but she stopped and looked at me. "Wait! He said bring your toothbrush too—does that mean you might not be coming back later today?"

"Yes! They might throw us in jail. I might have to spend the night there. But you know the plan. You stay at school till Miss Boone gets there, and then tell her I'm probably in jail. She'll tell our folks."

While I got my toothbrush, Georgia got me my sweater. "Here—wrap your sweater around your waist. It might get cool," she said in between tears.

"Don't be sad, Georgia. I am going to be okay."

"I want to march too, Rufus. I'd feel better if I was with you."

"I know, but you can't for this one. You heard what Uncle Sam said—one family member marches at a time. So you have to stay behind and be there to wipe Mama's tears tonight if I don't come home."

We hugged and ran out to Miss Boone's car.

Our drive to school was quiet. I didn't say much because I didn't want to lie to Miss Boone. Georgia was quiet too.

We jumped out of the car when we got to school and joined our circle of friends. Kids were making plans and organizing their food and toothbrushes in their pockets and little book bags.

"Here, take my sandwich too," Georgia said as she stuffed her sandwich in my pocket.

"Okay, Georgia, now you go on to class. I'll be okay."

She started to walk away but stopped and hugged me again.

"Love you," I whispered in her ear.

"Love you too. Please come back."

"I will. I promise," I said as I let her go and motioned for her to leave.

"Watch the clock. We leaving at noon," YouOut reminded us as we walked into the building. "We need to all get up at once and walk out. I'll stand up first. When we get to 16th Street Baptist, we go in the back door. They going to release us from the front door in groups of fifty."

"What if Miss Smith tries to stop us?" asked Sandy, a girl from Bull Hill. Slide had finally talked her into joining us.

"They ain't going to stop us," YouOut said. "The teachers are in on this thing too. They want their freedom just like we do."

"But if they try, just keep on walking," Ace added.

It was a long morning.

I kept looking at the clock.

Finally, both hands of the clock hit twelve.

YouOut stood up first.

Then Slide.

Then Ace.

Then me.

Miss Smith stood up from her desk. "I'm praying for all of you," she said as she watched us walk out of the classroom.

We followed YouOut down the hall.

Principal Mack was waiting for us at the front door.

"Be careful, children!" he said. "Come back here just like you left. I'm praying for you. We are all praying for you!" Then he disappeared behind the wooden door of his office as if he never saw us.

YouOut was right. The teachers were in on this too. We weren't going to need to sneak in or out of our school.

When I turned around, I could see more children behind us than I could count.

My heart was pounding as we got closer to 16th Street Baptist Church and ran into more and more students.

"Oh my God. Look at all these people," I said to Slide.

"So many! They must be coming from every school in Birmingham!" Slide said.

When we arrived at the church, we went in the back door, as we were instructed, and waited to be sent out in groups.

Finally it was our turn.

Yes, we walked in the back door, but we came out the front.

Down the steps we went!

"Sing," Ace reminded us as we crossed the street, and

he led us in song. *"Oh, freedom. Oh, freedom. Oh, freedom over me. And before I'd be a slave, I'd be buried in my grave."*

Ahead, I could make out Bull Connor standing in the middle of Kelly Park, next to the paddy wagons.

As we got closer, I could see the paddy wagon doors were open, and the police were pushing students inside.

"Ain't gonna let nobody turn me 'round, turn me 'round," we started to sing, but I realized that was exactly what Bull Connor was trying to do.

He looked as shocked as we were to see so many students.

In a few minutes, school buses began to arrive. Bull Connor must have ordered them so that he could load up children faster. But there were still too many of us! As soon as they'd fill up a bus, another group of students would run down the steps from 16th Street Baptist Church.

The children of Birmingham could not be stopped!

22

I stood at the edge of the park with Slide, YouOut, Ace, and the rest of my group, and we watched.

Cameramen were everywhere filming the action.

The police were getting tired, and we were getting stronger, as new students kept on arriving.

In a rage, Bull Connor ordered his men to clear the park, but it was almost impossible.

Soon the police started spreading out, trying to round us all up or get us to go home. They began pushing and shoving us so hard that kids started to fall to the ground.

Slide and I fell with force as two police officers

knocked us down, and I could feel my skin burning.

"You all right, dude?" It was Junie. He reached down and pulled me up.

"I'm okay."

"You guys should leave now. Go on back to school," Junie said. "We'll start over again tomorrow."

"We are staying!" Slide protested.

"No! I said go on back to school," Junie repeated. "They've run out of buses for now, but they'll return as soon as they drop the kids off at jail. Go back to school."

Me and Slide started walking to school, comparing wounds like we had been fighting in a battle. In all the confusion, we lost YouOut and Ace, but then I spotted Ace's sister, Angela.

"They arrested Ace and YouOut!" she told us. "They loaded them into the last bus. Our mama is going to be mad, and Miss Pearl will be mad when she finds out from Junie that YouOut is locked up."

Telling our parents what happened was a scary thought. But I didn't have to worry long about what I was going to tell mine, because when we got back to school, Daddy Paul was waiting, not Miss Boone. Georgia let go of his hands and ran to meet me. He ran behind her.

"I left the mill to pick you up. I knew it was too dangerous for Miss Boone to come downtown when we heard what was happening," Daddy Paul said as he wiped the dirt from my face. "Are you okay?"

"Yes, sir."

"Good. But I can't believe you didn't obey us."

"I am sorry, Daddy Paul, but I had to go. I just had to."

"Your mama's waiting for you. Let's go home."

"Is she real mad?"

"Yes. But mostly worried," Daddy Paul said. "She'll be glad to see you, but you might not be so glad to see her."

When we arrived home, I expected to see Mama come flying out of the house screaming and fussing at me, and I was right. There she was, standing on the porch, and she flew down the steps the moment she saw us. "Rufusssss . . . Lord, child. Are you all right?"

"I'm all right, Mama."

After she made sure I really was okay, she kissed my dirty face. "I told you to stay at school. You have not heard the end of this. Go take a bath, child. I will warm your food."

Georgia hugged me over and over again as she followed me inside.

Mama sat at the table with me as I ate everything on my plate.

"Son, did you know that over nine hundred children

are in jail tonight? You could have gone to jail too."

"I had to do it, Mama. I had to protest. You should've seen all of us. And if I land in jail, so be it."

"No, child. *No!* No jail! No more marching."

Mama was so mad that she got up and left the table. Daddy Paul followed her. I figured I was gonna be in big trouble, so I might as well enjoy my dinner. Georgia stayed in the kitchen with me and watched me eat a second plate of food.

After I ate and cleaned the kitchen, we went into the living room too.

Mama looked calmer. She turned the television off in the middle of the news.

"Rufus Jr., me and Paul been talking, and we got to put you on punishment. We ain't punishing you for marching. We are punishing you because you disobeyed us. You got to continue to do all of your chores, plus cut the grass all summer, and no television except for the news."

"All right, Mama," I said.

I didn't care about cartoons anymore. I definitely didn't want to watch Western movies anymore. We had our own fight! As long as I could watch the news, I'd be okay.

"I love you, son! I am sorry that you have to march for the freedom you should have," Mama said sadly.

"I know you think what you're doing is right, and it is—but you're still a child. I don't want you marching, so you can't go to school tomorrow. You and Georgia will stay home. I'll ask Frances and Maybell to check on you."

Mama was still holding my hand, but she reached over and turned the television back on with the other hand.

The reporter was talking about a man from the US Justice Department named Burke Marshall. He was coming to Birmingham with Attorney General Robert Kennedy.

Then they showed the jail all filled with kids. I looked closely at the television. Was that him? I wasn't quite sure, but . . . it did look like him.

"Mama, it's YouOut in the striped shirt! And that's Ace." I saw other students that I knew too.

They were all packed in the jail cells, and not one of them looked scared as they sang a freedom song. I could hear YouOut over everybody.

We shall overcome
We shall overcome
We shall overcome someday
Oh, deep in my heart, I do believe
We shall overcome someday.

We are not afraid
We are not afraid
We are not afraid today
Oh, deep in my heart, I do believe
We are not afraid today.

Mama turned off the television and gave me another kiss on the forehead.

I looked around the room at the people who loved me. I looked at Georgia, holding her little white doll because Mama could not find any colored dolls. I wanted my little sister to have a doll that looked like her. I wanted her to go to the amusement park one day.

There was no way I would not return to Kelly Park tomorrow.

Mama would be mad and upset that I lied to them and said I'd stay home—but it was just like how Mama had to lie to Georgia about Kiddieland. I had to protect our family. I wanted to protect our future. Lying did not feel as bad as drinking from the "colored" water fountain and watching my folks walking in and out of back doors the rest of their lives.

If the children of Birmingham were going to jail, I was going too!

23

"Okay, Georgia, this is my plan," I told her after Mama and Daddy Paul left for work the next morning. "I am going to walk to Kelly Park, and I need you to stay here. Don't open the door for nobody except Miss Boone or Miss Maybell."

"If they come over, what do I tell them?" Georgia asked.

"By the time they come, I will be gone, so you don't have to lie. If I don't come home by four or five, you'll know I am in jail."

"You know I wish I could go," Georgia said.

"I know you want to march, little sister, but not

today. It's too dangerous. Promise me you'll stay here. Don't follow me."

"I promise," Georgia said as we went into the kitchen to make sandwiches. I turned on the radio to hear what DJ Shelley had to say.

"Well, folks, today the party is starting early, so let's go. And it may go real late, so you know what to do!" DJ Shelley said before playing another song.

Yes, I know what to do.

I put my sandwich and the extra one Georgia made for me in my deep pocket.

Out the back door I went so that Miss Boone and Miss Maybell would not see me. I ran down the steps and across the backyard. I stopped and turned around to make sure Georgia was not following me. I realized I was standing in the spot where the white men had burned the cross.

Georgia was looking at me standing in the spot. "Run, Rufus, run!" she said through the screen door.

I stepped off the charred grass and ran as fast as I could.

In a few blocks, when I got out of the white neighborhood and onto Simmons Road, I could not believe my eyes.

Colored children were everywhere. They were on their way to Kelly Park.

I saw Slide and Sandy when I arrived at 16th Street Baptist Church.

"No need to go inside the church. It's full," Slide said.

"Who else came from our school?" I asked.

"I don't know. We walked from Bull Hill. They didn't send any buses today. They need them to take us to jail. Mama and Daddy told me to stay home anyway, but I ran off as soon as she went to work."

"I ran off soon as my folks went to work too, but Bull Hill is eighteen miles from here! I can't believe y'all walked."

"For our freedom—you better believe it! Let's go!" Sandy said.

Just like the day before, students kept pouring out of 16th Street Baptist Church.

As we filled the park, we could hear the dogs barking, and the fire trucks even louder. The firemen jumped out and grabbed their hoses.

We could see Bull Connor giving the firemen orders with his hands.

They gave us one warning: "Leave or we will turn on the hoses."

We kept on marching!

Bull Connor turned around and looked at us.

I looked into his eyes.

I looked at the firemen.

I looked at the fire hoses in their hands.

But there was no fire.

Then it hit me.

We were the fire!

Ol' Bull Connor raised both arms like he was parting the Red Sea.

"Let 'em have it," he shouted.

The water shocked our bodies and knocked some children down.

Junie ran over to help us and called out his own orders.

"Keep marching. They ain't going to kill us on live TV. Keep marching!"

YouOut's big brother had this look in his eyes like an old soul ready to meet his maker.

Slide and I ran against the water to get next to Junie. If we were going down, we were going together.

We moved in closer, but Bull Connor was not finished with us. "Turn it up. Turn it up!" he shouted.

"Freedom, oh, freedom!" we shouted back.

The fireman turned the pressure up so high that it threw us into the air like paper dolls.

They are *going to kill us all,* I thought as the water started to burn my body.

We landed on the ground just long enough to catch

our breath before the water started washing us down the pavement.

Before I knew it, I landed against the tire of a school bus.

I looked up and saw police boots. A foot lifted to kick me but stopped as a photographer started to flash his camera in the policeman's face.

The officer grabbed me up hard and threw me inside the school bus. I couldn't see Slide anywhere as they packed us into the bus like sardines.

I glanced across the street at the 16th Street Baptist Church. The church my mama loved, where she went as a little girl.

I looked at the children still coming out of the church. They could see us getting beaten, but they kept on coming. Kept running down the steps. Kept running for our freedom.

24

"Where are they taking us?" Sandy asked as she stood beside me on the crowded bus. "We just passed the downtown jail."

I turned around and answered, "I don't know."

No one knew until we arrived at the fairgrounds. It turned out the jails were full, so they packed us into the pens they used for animals during the state fair.

"Anyone seen Slide?" I asked Sandy.

"Back here," I heard Slide say as he made his way near us.

I looked around at all the children packed inside the pens. Some were still soaking wet. Some were crying.

I thought about Mama. I knew she was worried. I thought about Ace and YouOut, who were in jail downtown. And where was Junie? I had no idea if he got away or was herded onto a different bus.

I reached in my pocket to share my sandwiches with my friends, but that pocket was empty. The sandwiches must have fallen out in Kelly Park, and I hadn't even realized it. My toothbrush was gone too.

We sat on the ground and waited—we weren't even sure for what.

"When do they feed us?" asked a little boy who looked to be only around eight.

"Feed us? Sometimes they do, but sometimes they don't," a teenager told him.

The little boy started to cry.

"Here, take this. What's your name?" Slide asked as he gave the boy a candy bar that looked like it had been in his pocket for months.

"My name is Jimmy," he said as he ate the candy. That made him happy for a few minutes, but soon Jimmy started to cry again. "I don't know what happened to my sister."

"Don't worry, it's going to be all right," I told him.

Slide looked down at him. "Sing with us, Jimmy."

"Freedom, oh, freedom," we all sang, and Jimmy joined in.

Soon some colored workers arrived with our dinner.

I watched the grown-ups across from us passing their food to the children to make sure we had enough to eat. I gave Jimmy my crackers, and he looked up and smiled at me as I pretended the cold pork-and-beans in a can were good.

When we finished eating, the singing started again.

As I sang, I thought about Mama. I could hear her voice singing to me all my life. I knew she was at home praying for her child. I prayed that she wouldn't worry too much. I knew Daddy Paul would comfort my mama and Georgia.

It seemed everybody was worried about someone tonight.

We sang until we fell asleep one by one.

25

The sound of men talking woke us up the next
morning.

"Get back, get back," the policemen shouted as they
hit the fence with their billy clubs to make us move back
even farther so they could pack more children into the
animal pens.

That is when we realized the children had returned
to Kelly Park for a third day of marching.

Every time they put someone new in the pen, they'd
give us an update. We learned that the jails downtown
were filled with mostly children. Thousands of children.

"Hey, Scott," I said when I saw Ace's friend from

the football team thrown into the pen with us.

"Hey, man, y'all all right?" he asked.

"We good. What's going on in Kelly Park?"

"Everything! Students from all over Birmingham are still protesting in the park, and things are getting bad down there. Another student was bitten by a dog today, and I heard the bus driver say they are bringing in the National Guard if things don't calm down."

It was almost noon when they finally gave us breakfast. Breakfast that was worse than dinner the night before. The biscuits were as hard as a brick, and the sausage was as dry as a bone.

Jimmy watched me take a bite.

"Yummy!" I said with a smile.

"You can't fool me, Rufus! That biscuit looks like dog food!"

"Yep! And it taste like dog food too, but we have to eat. I'll take another bite, will you?"

"Okay," Jimmy said, and we made time pass taking small bite after small bite.

After breakfast we started to sing again, and the jailer tried to make us stop.

The more they yelled at us, the louder we sang. Just like we had outnumbered them in Kelly Park, we outnumbered them in their own jails. We sang the rest of the day.

It was starting to get dark when I heard them call "Rufus," "Curtis," "Sandy," and the names of other kids from Bull Hill. Thank God they called Jimmy's name, because I didn't want to leave him.

"Slide, we are going home!" I said as we jumped up.

We waved goodbye to our cellmates, and I felt bad about leaving them behind as we ran to the front gate.

Mamas and daddies were standing outside waiting for their children. I watched as little Jimmy jumped into his daddy's arms. He waved at us as I ran toward Daddy Paul and Uncle Sam. Slide's daddy was there too, and so was Sandy's mom, Miss Lucy Ellen.

They were so happy to see us.

"There are still hundreds of children in there, maybe thousands," I told my uncle and Daddy Paul as soon as I got in the car.

"We know. It's on the national news."

"How are Mama and Georgia? What about Miss Maybell and Miss Boone?" I asked.

"They are fine, son, and they proud of you. But of course, you know your mama is real upset."

"I know, I know, and I'm sorry," I told Daddy Paul, and it made me feel good that he looked at me like he understood. "Do you know what happened to YouOut and Ace?"

"YouOut and Ace were released, but they are still

holding Junie and some of the teenagers. But don't worry; they'll get out of jail soon. Folks are making their rounds to bail out as many children as possible before nightfall."

"What's going to happen next? What are they saying on the news?" I asked.

"A picture of one of the students being bit by a dog went out on the nightly news. I think a lot of people are shocked at what's happening to you kids here in Birmingham. That fellow from the Justice Department arrived, and he's talking to the white business leaders and the Southern Christian Leadership Conference."

"Why do the white businessmen care that we are in jail?" I asked.

"Oh, they care, child," Daddy Paul said. "Big companies don't want to do business with a town that beats children and attack them with dogs—no matter what their color. They like their money more than they like Bull Connor. They are not going to stand by and watch him let Birmingham explode."

I listened for a minute and said, "So that means the children marching is working. It's working, Daddy Paul. Tell me that it's working."

"Yes, son, it is working. No doubt that it's working."

26

Mama wasn't standing on the porch this time when I got home, so I jumped out of the car and ran through the screen door.

I could see her sitting on the couch with her head down, crying. Aunt Ola and Georgia were sitting with her like it was the end of the world.

Mama looked up and saw me, but she didn't move, so I ran over to her and put my head on her lap. I breathed in her lavender perfume. "Mama, Mama . . . don't cry. I am home."

"Son!" she said as she wrapped her arms around me and whispered in my ear, "Mama loves you."

"I love you too, Mama."

When she let go, she looked at me.

"You all right?"

"Yes, ma'am. I am sorry I ran off, Mama, but I had to. I just had to."

"We will talk about that later. I am just glad you all right. I'm glad you're alive."

"Me too, Mama. Me too!"

She rubbed my hair and looked at me like it was the first time she'd ever seen me. Then she smiled. "You smell terrible, child. Are you hungry?"

"Yes, Mama, I'm real hungry."

"Go take a good bath, and by the time you're out the tub, I'll have dinner ready," Mama said.

"I'll help you, Mama. Let me help!" Georgia said. She was about to give me a hug but stopped. "Boy, you stink! I'll wait till you bathe." Georgia let out a big laugh, and I wished I could laugh too, but I just wasn't feeling it.

I went to the bathroom and turned on the bath.

I looked in the mirror and finally let out all the tears I'd been holding back for days.

When the tub was full, I got in and lay there, letting the water soothe my body. I wanted to wash the hate of Bull Connor and his men off me. I could not get the smell of the fairgrounds off my soul.

When I was all clean, I went to the living room and was surprised to see Miss Boone and Miss Maybell sitting there.

"We came to see about you, Rufus," Miss Boone explained as she got up and hugged me real tight. No white person had ever hugged me before, but I didn't mind, so I hugged her back. And then Miss Maybell hugged me too.

"I am real proud of you, Rufus. I always knew you were noble." Miss Boone winked at me, then turned to my mama. "Well, we best be going. We just wanted to make sure everything worked out. We're so glad Rufus is okay."

As soon as our company left, I sat down and started to eat.

"Slow down. You going to choke!" Mama said as I devoured the smothered chicken.

"Here, child, drink a little tea. That's too much food in your mouth," Aunt Ola added.

"But it's so good!" I managed to say between bites. "Thanks! They practically starved us in that jail."

Uncle Sam and Daddy Paul hadn't said anything while the women fussed over me, but now Daddy Paul said, "Tell your mama thank you."

I was confused. "I just did."

"No, he means for bailing you out of jail," Uncle

Sam said. "It was your mama who bailed out you and Slide and your friends from Bull Hill. She also bailed out plenty of kids she didn't know."

"Thank you, Mama! That was so good of you."

"You know I'd do anything for you and your friends, child. And . . . for the movement too."

"We all appreciate what you and Paul are doing, sister," Uncle Sam said to my mama.

Mama smiled at her big brother. Watching them made me think that they loved each other like me and Georgia loved each other. It felt so good to be sitting here with my family. I was home and I was safe again. I now understood Mama's wanting to keep us safe.

"It's late, Sam," Mama told her brother. "Y'all stay here tonight. Rufus can sleep on the sofa in the living room."

"Yes, please stay. You can sleep in my room," I added.

They agreed to stay, and as everyone got up, Mama reminded me that it was my night to do the dishes. Jail or no jail, Mama was not letting me off the hook with my chores.

But I was glad to be alone in the kitchen so I could listen to the radio. I was hoping to hear DJ Shelley, and when I turned the radio on, his voice was the first thing I heard.

"Well, it's been a long day, folks," he said. *"I just wanted to come back on the radio to say good night. I've been rocking and rolling all day long, but so have the children of Birmingham. That's right! The children of Birmingham are our heroes, and you better believe that."*

When I was done with the dishes, I turned the radio off and went outside to sit on the back steps.

It was dark, so I couldn't see the black spot where they burned the cross in our yard, but I knew it was there. It was there just like segregation in Birmingham. We might not always see it, but it was there.

Maybe the children marching had put out a little of their fire, just like Daddy Paul did with the burning cross.

"You all right?" Daddy Paul said from the doorway.

"I'm all right. Just thinking."

"Come on inside soon. It's ain't safe out here," he added.

"Ain't no place in Birmingham safe for us, right?"

"That's true, son, but because of brave children like you, things are going to change," he said as he opened the door and came out onto the porch.

"I hope you're right. I keep thinking about all that happened in Kelly Park."

"I can tell you what happened. Over three thousand colored children rose up to show the world they won't stand for injustice. That it's past time to fix a racist system. And the whole world was watching, Rufus. It really was. You were one of those children, and I'm so proud of you."

I got up to stand next to him and said, "Thank you, Daddy."

"Daddy?" My stepdaddy put his arm around me.

"Yes, sir, Daddy." No man could ever take my real daddy's place, but having Daddy Paul to love us made all the difference in our lives. I wanted him to know that.

The back door opened again, and this time Mama and Georgia came out.

"I thought you two were in bed," I said.

"We were putting sheets on the sofa for you," Mama said. I could see her smiling. I knew she had heard me say "Daddy."

"I'm gonna call you Daddy too," Georgia said.

"That'd be real nice, Georgia. Real nice indeed," Daddy said as he put his other arm around Georgia.

Georgia pointed to the sky. "Look! It's a falling star. Make a wish, everyone. Make a wish."

I closed my eyes and made a wish.

"What was your wish, Rufus?" Georgia asked. "I know you're not supposed to tell, but please tell me. Please, please?"

"I wished for a better world for you, little sister. A better world for all of us. Where we're all treated the same."

We all stood together for a while and looked up at the sky. I thought about all the children in Kelly Park as the stars shined brightly over Birmingham.

AUTHOR'S NOTE

Even though *We Were the Fire* is historical fiction, the truth is on every page. The truth about what happened to the children of Birmingham in 1963. The truth about who they were and what they endured. Stories about people who were left out of our history books and legendary stories about the civil rights movement. The famous and nameless warriors all have a place in history that we must seek to find. This book ends on May 4, 1963, for a reason. I wanted you to know what happened and what led up to the Civil Rights Act of 1964, the Voting Rights Act of 1965, and so many historic moments that shaped this country and changed the world.

It is also important to know that the marching did not end on "Double D-Day." The children of Birmingham refused to go home until they broke the back of the city and maybe this country.

For two days, the children were washed down the streets, beaten by the police, and bitten by dogs, yet they still returned to Kelly Ingram Park on May 4, and they were ready to join the three thousand children already in jail.

By May 10, the police and the City of Birmingham were so worn down by the children, they came to an agreement with Dr. King and the other leaders. The agreement included removal of all "Whites Only" and "Colored Only" signs in restrooms and on drinking fountains. This agreement also included a plan to desegregate lunch counters and schools. More jobs were promised to African Americans, and all the protesters who were in jail were released immediately. It was not written in the agreement, but the day before the agreement was signed, Bull Connor was fired.

The adults and children were happy about the agreement and the firing of Connor, but segregationists in Birmingham were furious. They were so outraged that they bombed the A. G. Gaston Motel and the home of Reverend A. D. King on the same night. The violence forced President John F. Kennedy to send in three thousand federal troops.

The city was once again a city of rage, and the situation escalated when the Board of Education announced on May 20 that over one thousand children were expelled from school for participating in the marches. Dr. King had left town but rushed back to Birmingham when he received the news and promised they would return to Kelly Park if the children were not readmitted to their schools immediately. On May 22, all the students went to school, and they rejoiced.

As the school year ended and the children left Kelly Park, the pain of the movement shifted to Mississippi. On June 5, Medgar Evers was gunned down in his driveway. He left behind a wife, four children, and people around the country who dreamed of their freedom.

On August 28, 1963, Dr. King, Dick Gregory, A. Philip Randolph, Andrew Young, John Lewis, Diane Nash, and the men and women of Birmingham loaded their children into their vehicles and went to the March on Washington to talk about their dreams. Over 500,000 people showed up that day, and they went home with hope. That hope faded on September 15, when four beautiful little girls went to 16th Street Baptist Church and didn't come home. The KKK bombed 16th Street Baptist Church, killing Addie Mae Collins, Denise McNair, Carole Robinson, and Cynthia Morris Wesley. Addie Collins's sister Sarah was seriously injured, and other members suffered burns and cuts. In addition to this horror, the history books have somehow left out the names of two teenagers who also died on September 15. Hours after the bombing, as the sun set in Birmingham, a teenage Black boy named Virgil Ware, who was only thirteen, was shot by a white teen named Larry Sims. Larry Sims only served six months in a juvenile detention center. Johnny Robinson was killed by a white police officer who claimed Johnny threw a rock at him. The officer was never charged, and their stories are rarely mentioned.

As the country and people around the world cried for our children and Medgar Evers, President Kennedy was assassinated on November 22, 1963. To some, all the deaths make 1963 feel like a year of mourning, and in many ways it was. Most of all, it was a year of triumphs. The year children challenged the system and won.

One hundred years from now, people will talk about what happened in Birmingham in 1963. The real historians will tell the real truth about a city that children brought to its knees. They have a moral obligation to go back and reexamine what happened in Birmingham. They will have to talk about the children who changed the course of history. The children who were the fire!

ACKNOWLEDGMENTS

There are no words to express my gratitude as I witness this book enter the world. I am so grateful to my wonderful editor, Nancy Paulsen. The truth is, I struggled to find my voice after surviving stage 3 breast cancer. When I was ready, Nancy and her staff were standing at the door with a welcome sign.

Every writer should have a few honest people to read their manuscripts in between rounds with their editor. I have Crystal Moses and Yvonne Irvin. Thank you, ladies!

My mother is with our ancestors now, but thank

you, Ma, for being the first writer in this family and giving me the courage to tell stories that are important.

Thank God for my siblings and their spouses, who read my first book when no one else would! What could I do without real friends like Sandy Washington, Marie Showers, D'anne Goins, Stephanie Ponteau, Deborah Rogers, and Agnes Boykins.

And last but not least, I am thankful to Dick Gregory and the children of Birmingham. It was Dick Gregory who gave me a front seat to history and told me his experience in Birmingham in 1963. He told me what the newspapers did not write and what the television did not broadcast. He made me see what others refused to see about thousands of brave Black children who stood up to racism and Bull Connor in Kelly Ingram Park.

To you, the children of Birmingham: Your bravery was not in vain. The little soldiers who sacrificed on the battlefield of Birmingham . . . your living was not in vain. Neither the water from the hoses, the fire at the church, harsh words, nor death will erase what you did for us! For that, I say thank you.